He kissed her hard, forcing her lips open

When Gordon released her, he grinned. "Very inexperienced, but I like the way you try to kiss. If I gave you some tuition, you could be very good."

Fiona stared at him, her bosom heaving. Then she said tauntingly, "I know why you make fun of kissing me. You're afraid you mightn't be able to—control yourself. I'm right, aren't I?"

Laughing sardonically, Gordon retorted, "My dear child, I've had sexier females than you try their wiles on me."

"That may be," she countered, triumph in her voice, "but you're the one who shoved me away in the end. You're scared!"

Gordon took a pace forward and grabbed her in his arms. "Okay," he growled, "you asked for it. Just don't start screaming when you get it!"

WELCOME
TO THE WONDERFUL WORLD
OF *Harlequin Romances*

Interesting, informative and entertaining,
each Harlequin Romance portrays an appealing
and original love story. With a varied array
of settings, we may lure you on an African safari,
to a quaint Welsh village, or an exotic Riviera
location—anywhere and everywhere that adventurous
men and women fall in love.

As publishers of Harlequin Romances, we're
extremely proud of our books. Since 1949,
Harlequin Enterprises has built its publishing
reputation on the solid base of quality and
originality. Our stories are the most popular
paperback romances sold in North America: every
month, six new titles are released and sold at
nearly every book-selling store in Canada and the
United States.

A free catalogue listing all Harlequin Romances
can be yours by writing to the

HARLEQUIN READER SERVICE,
(In the U.S.) 1440 South Priest Drive, Tempe, AZ 85281
(In Canada) Stratford, Ontario N5A 6W2

We sincerely hope you enjoy reading
this Harlequin Romance.

Yours truly,

THE PUBLISHERS
Harlequin Romances

Highlands Rapture

by

DIANA GAIR

Harlequin Books

TORONTO • NEW YORK • LOS ANGELES • LONDON
AMSTERDAM • PARIS • SYDNEY • HAMBURG
STOCKHOLM • ATHENS • TOKYO • MILAN

Original hardcover edition published in 1982
by Mills & Boon Limited

ISBN 0-373-02519-X

Harlequin Romance first edition December 1982

CHAPTER ONE

Tartan skirt flying, Fiona Cameron ran for her life over the springy purple heather that dappled the rocky Scottish hillside. Her long red hair streamed in the wind that sang through a clump of tall pine trees just ahead. Beyond the trees she could see a broad, winding stream, or burn as they were called in Scotland, and she thought if she reached the burn she could follow it downstream until she came to a bridge, where there would be a road. Then she could probably hitch a ride and escape the angry deer-shooters who were pursuing her.

In one hand she clutched a large red firecracker which was the last of six she had carried when she had set out with her friends to disrupt the opening of the deer shooting at Sir Angus Deardon's Duntochter Castle estate. And disrupt it they certainly had, she thought gleefully as her shapely legs in grey knee-length stockings and brown brogues carried her over the peaty turf towards the pines and the burn.

Nearer the burn, the ground became boggy, with scattered pools of brown water which she leapt nimbly over until she came to two larger pools flanking a thicket of bracken. As she raced along, she debated whether to jump over one of the pools, then realised it was too wide. Instead, she veered suddenly and plunged straight through the thicket. She gave a squeal of fright as she tumbled head over heels into a shallow pit that the bushes concealed. The pit was occupied by a large, fair-haired man and what seemed to be a whole studio full of camera equipment, tripods and carry cases.

The man grunted and exploded into a vigorous oath as she landed on top of him, winding him, and for a moment the pit was a muddy, thrashing jumble as he writhed under her flailing body as she tried to scramble to her feet to continue her flight.

Then two strong hands gripped her shoulders and he thrust her off his body, then rose to his feet, pulling her up as he did so.

She stood panting and looked up at him in his Harris tweed jacket with leather at the elbows and his red polo-neck sweater and brown cord pants. His fair hair was dishevelled, and like hers, it had sprigs of heather in it and there was some mud on his face. He had smouldering grey eyes, and at any other time she would have thought he had a nice face—strong-featured, with a hawkish nose and a square, determined chin. He looked Scandinavian, so she was surprised when he spoke with an American accent.

'Where the hell do you think you're going?' he growled, his gaze taking in her flaming red hair and angry green eyes as she struggled in his grasp. Then he looked at the firecracker she was still clutching in one hand.

'Are you one of the idiots who threw the fire-works?' he snapped. 'You look like the mad bomber! Not that you need a bomb to wreck things. God knows what you've done to my cameras!'

He glanced at the photographic equipment that had been thrown around the pit by her onslaught. Then he gave her a shake. 'I won't say how many thousands of bucks this gear is worth. But I sure hope you've got enough to pay for any damage!'

Fiona struggled in his grasp. 'Let me go!' she cried. 'It was an accident! How was I to know you were lying behind the bushes?'

He raised one eyebrow, surprised. 'Oh, so you're not a Scottish lassie? You sound English. What are you doing in the Highlands—disrupting a perfectly legal deer shoot?'

'I'm a New Zealander,' she said shortly, 'but I'm of Scottish descent. And I'm concerned about wild animals being murdered in the name of sport.'

He rolled his eyes. 'And you came all the way from New Zealand to—to register your protest?'

'No!' she snapped. 'I'm here on holiday. Now will you let me go?'

She glanced fearfully over her shoulder as she struggled in his grip.

He scowled and his grey eyes stayed frosty as he surveyed her. 'I guess you don't want to be caught by Sir Angus or his gamekeepers or his guests—of whom, by the way, I'm one.'

'Oh!' she exclaimed, 'so you're with the shooting party?'

He shook his head. 'I'm a photographer. The only shooting I aimed to do was with my camera.

But you and your protesting friends broke up the shoot—and it looks as if you may have broken my cameras. Not a bad day's work! I'd say you're going to be in trouble—when Sir Angus and his men get here.'

'Then let me go!' Fiona cried, struggling to free herself from his vice-like grip on her shoulders.

'Give me one good reason why I should?' he said sternly as he held her at arm's length. 'You've disrupted my host's sport. You're trespassing on his estate—and you've ruined a photographic assignment I came three thousand miles to shoot. I spent days picking this spot and digging this hide to catch the action. Can you give me one good reason why I shouldn't hold you until Sir Angus and his gamekeepers arrive?'

'Yes,' she mumbled. 'I—I've hurt my ankle, and I want to bathe it in the burn. It—it's sore.'

He thrust her out to arm's length, then studied her, his eyes straying down to her shapely ankle in its sturdy brogue.

'You're all dirty,' he growled, surveying her dishevelled figure as she stood mutinously before him.

Fiona glanced quickly down at her pink angora wool sweater and red Cameron tartan skirt. She was covered in mud from the peaty soil of the pit.

She looked apprehensively over her shoulder, uphill across the heather in the direction she had come from. But, amazingly, there was no sign of pursuit. After they had disrupted the deer shoot, Fiona and the three men she had been with had all dashed away in different directions. She guessed that Sir Angus, his gamekeepers and guests must have decided to concentrate on chasing the three men. But she felt sure Charles, Hamish and Colin would easily outrun the shooters, who wore heavy tweeds and shooting jackets and carried haversacks and guns. Fiona had found no difficulty keeping ahead of the two men who had chased her. Her only fear was that they would get so angry that they might shoot at her. But they hadn't. So now all she had to do was get away from this domineering American and she would be able to go downstream and eventually make it safely back to Elgin House where she was staying with Charles Stewart and his mother.

She brushed some mud from her skirt and said in a small voice, 'I'd like to clean up a little. Can I go down to the burn?'

'O.K.,' he said, taking his hands from her shoulders. 'But first tell me your name.'

Instinctively, she almost told him, then she checked herself and said, 'It's Mary—Mary MacDonald.'

He looked at her searchingly and she avoided his eyes. He grunted, 'You'd be the poorest liar I've ever met. Now, what's your real name? Come on, out with it—a New Zealand girl in the Highlands wouldn't be too hard to track down. Especially one with red hair and green eyes who looks as if she only left school last year.'

She flushed and said curtly, 'It's Fiona—Fiona Cameron.'

He nodded. 'I'm Gordon Ross. From Boston, Massachusetts.'

'I guessed you were American,' she said shortly.

'And what age are you? You look about six-teen.'

'I'm nineteen,' she said indignantly. 'And I'm going now.'

One hand shot out and he gripped her arm. 'Not so fast. Where are you staying?'

'Why do you want to know?' she retorted.

He shrugged. 'Sir Angus might want to.'

She stared. 'You wouldn't tell him! You said you're not a shooter. I haven't spoiled your fun—or sport, as they call it.'

He smiled frostily. 'I told you I was planning to photograph the deer shoot. You've caused a couple of days' work to go up the creek. You could say I'm just as angry as Sir Angus. I've no reason to let you get away scot free.'

'But you will,' she said, trying a wheedling tone. 'I'm sure your cameras are all right. And you don't want me to get arrested, do you?'

He grunted. 'I'm not too sure about that. You do-gooders are a pain in the neck sometimes. Can't you find something better to do than spoil the peace of these lovely Highlands?'

Her face creased with indignation. 'We don't spoil the peace! It's the shooters who do that! Killing helpless animals—for sport!' She almost spat her contempt.

He raised his eyes wearily. 'O.K., O.K., I've been through this a hundred times. Tell me where you live and I'll let you go.'

Fiona said shortly that she was staying with

Mrs Jessie Stewart at Elgin House outside Duntochter village.

Gordon Ross nodded. 'I know the place. And what are the names of your friends who were throwing the firecrackers and stampeding the deer? I saw some of them running away before you came crashing on top of me.'

'I'm not going to tell you,' she said vehemently. 'You've no right to ask me that!'

'I've got every right,' he said coldly. 'I might want to interview them. Concerned ecologists— whatever they are. I'm a photo-journalist. I write words as well as take pictures.'

'You want their names so you can tell Sir Angus!' she flashed. 'Well, I'm not going to tell you. I bet they managed to get away all right, so I'm not going to say who they are!'

She glared at him defiantly, her eyes snapping.

He scowled. 'Then I guess I might have to hold you here—how does that grab you?'

'Not very much,' she said shortly, wriggling in his grip. 'I'd like to go.'

He put his free hand under her chin, which she wrenched away. He smiled mockingly, 'Right, then say please—nicely—and I might let you go.'

'No!' she cried hotly, 'I won't say please! You've no right to hold me here! You're just a— a damned bully! So let me go!'

'Please?' he teased.

'No!'

He frowned and shook his head. 'You're a stubborn little spitfire! Your boy-friend must find you a regular handful!'

Fiona twisted her arm in his grip. 'I haven't got a boy-friend, and I—I——' She let her head droop and her slim body sag. 'I want to go,' she said in the humblest tone she could muster. 'I'm all muddy and wet. I—I want to go home.'

Gordon Ross bent his head, trying to peer under her tangled red hair at her face. 'Did I hear please?'

Suddenly she struck at his hand holding her arm and simultaneously shoved him hard, and he stumbled and fell back.

She broke free and cried triumphantly, 'No, you didn't hear please! And now you can go to blazes!'

She turned and ran like the wind towards the burn and the stepping stones, and as she ran she risked a quick glance over her shoulder and saw that he was pounding after her. As she ran she realised that this was no middle-aged deer-shooter chasing her, but a man in his early thirties and in excellent physical condition.

She reached the slippery, moss-covered stepping stones and leapt lightly on to the first slab, then on to the second, when she heard his heavy breathing. She glanced round and gave a startled gasp when she saw he was almost upon her. In her heavy and unfamiliar brogues, one foot slipped on the mossy stone and she teetered, trying to maintain her balance when she heard him yell, 'You dumb nut, you'll break your neck! I'll——'

She heard no more as her foot skidded down the side of the slippery stone, then with an anguished squeal she plunged face first into the brown swirling water on the deep side.

It was cold and wet, but only about four feet deep. Gasping and spluttering, Fiona thrashed her way to the surface and spat water as she found a footing on the slippery bottom. Her sense of physical shock was superseded by outrage and fury as she splashed with her arms to stay afloat as she stared up at Gordon Ross.

He knelt and surveyed her, only her head and shoulders visible above the brown water, her red hair plastered in wet strands around her scarlet face. He said casually, 'You look like a drowned rat.'

She slapped the water furiously with the flat of both hands. 'It was your *fault*!' she cried.

He shrugged. 'I didn't shove you in, you slipped. You were running too fast.'

'I was running because you were chasing me! You're a damned great *bully*!'

He scowled, then said conversationally, 'You planning to stay in there?'

'No!' she spat. 'But remember, if I catch pneumonia, it'll be your fault!'

He shrugged. 'It's a beautiful day. You'll soon dry out.' He stretched out one hand. 'Here—I'll help you.'

'No, thank you!' she said savagely, 'I'll help myself.'

She began half walking, half swimming towards the far bank until she reached shallow water when she waded dripping through clinging reeds and water lilies up the shelving bank and stood on white pebbles. She shook herself like a dog and water sprayed from her dripping figure. Her sweater had moulded itself to her body and her skirt stuck to her thighs as she stood, her brogues squelching, oozing water.

Gordon Ross strolled across the stepping stones and surveyed her, then said, 'You look like a slinky otter, not a rat.'

'Thank you,' she said, her voice low and furious, 'That must make you feel very good.'

He shrugged. 'It was your own fault. But I won't leave you to walk home. Hang on until I pack the gear into my Land Rover, then I'll give you a ride.'

'No, thanks!' she said scornfully, tossing her wet head. 'I'd rather walk.'

She turned, her brogues squelching on the pebbles, and strode up the bank on to the heather.

As she stalked across the peaty turf she was glad it was a warm day. Some of the chill she had felt when she got out of the water disappeared as she strode vigorously through the heather and bog myrtle. Her rage helped warm her quivering body as she strode along, following the course of the burn.

Gordon Ross was just the kind of arrogant, domineering male she disliked. He hadn't been at all concerned when she'd toppled into the water—she could have hurt herself for all he knew, but all she'd seen in his eyes was amusement as he looked down at her. She supposed he felt it had been poetic justic. She had helped disrupt his host's deer shoot, then knocked over his precious cameras—and she'd got a ducking in her haste to escape from him. He was a cowardly bully, she thought wrathfully as she squelched through the heather.

And yet there had been something about him that made her wish she had met him under different circumstances. Not that leaping on top of him and knocking him over could be considered a proper meeting—certainly not a formal introduction. She remembered his hands on her shoulders and the effortless way he had lifted her to her feet after she had landed on him. If he had wanted to, he could have shaken the life out of her—but he hadn't, although he'd been rough enough.

As she strode on, Fiona mellowed slightly. She supposed she was lucky she'd got away from him. He could have held her and handed her over to Sir Angus.

Ah well, she consoled herself, you had to take some risks when you went out on an anti-blood sports crusade. These sort of hunters and shooters weren't above beating up people like her who deliberately disrupted their sport. She thought about Charles Stewart and his friends Hamish and Colin who had planned the disruption of Sir Angus's deer hunt—or deer slaughter. Like her, they were dedicated conservationists and very concerned about wild life and the environment. She had been proud that they had accepted her into their group and let her come on the deer operation. Although Charles had had some misgivings about involving a visitor, especially a girl, in their plans.

But Charles had known her for over a year now, almost from when she had first come to London from Auckland. He knew how she felt about the killing of defenceless animals in the name of sport. She thought he was a very nice person, streets ahead of Gordon Ross. She bet that if Charles had been with her then Gordon Ross wouldn't have been able to manhandle her as he had done.

She heard the low throb of a motor and glanced over her shoulder to see a Land Rover bumping its way across the heather, following her.

She heard Gordon Ross's voice raised above the sound of the motor, 'You're not going to get anywhere walking in that direction—you've got a ten-mile hike before you reach a road. Get in and I'll run you back to your house.'

Fiona tossed her head and squelched on determinedly through the heather.

She heard the Land Rover suddenly accelerate and it shot across her path, blocking her, then it squealed to a halt. Gordon Ross slid from behind the wheel and stood in her path.

She tried to move around him, but he stepped in front of her. 'Come on,' he said, 'get in. I'll have you home in half an hour.'

'No, thank you!' she said savagely. 'I wouldn't ride with you under any circumstances!'

He grunted, then abruptly picked her up in his arms, and, kicking and protesting, she was carried around the Land Rover and he held her while he opened the passenger door, then unceremoniously bundled her inside. There was a squelching sound from her wet skirt as he forced her to sit on the seat, then he slammed the door shut while she glared at him furiously.

She decided it wasn't worth trying to jump out, for he'd probably only chase her and catch her and force her back into the car. He seemed determined to humiliate her and play the domineering, masterful male. But in fact, she was rather glad he had forced her to accept the ride, for she'd begun to feel chilly in the slight breeze that had sprung up in the October afternoon.

Gordon Ross got in behind the wheel and slammed his door shut then put the vehicle in gear and turned it in a wide circle and drove slowly across the heather.

She could feel him glancing at her occasionally, but she said nothing and hung on to the dashboard as the Land Rover bumped across the rough moorland.

Then he asked briefly, 'This your first visit to Scotland?'

'Yes,' she said shortly.

'Visiting the land of your ancestors?'

'Yes. My father's family came from round here. And so did my mother's—from farther north, near Braeside.'

He said, 'I've got some Scottish blood too, a long way back. But I guess yours is more recent.'

'Yes. My grandparents emigrated to New Zealand from Scotland.'

'And what kind of work do you do in New Zealand?'

'I don't work in New Zealand. I came to

London a year ago. I'm with the B.B.C., in radio.'

'What branch?'

'Programme continuity. I did the same kind of job in Auckland.'

'So this is a working vacation?'

She nodded. 'More or less. Every New Zealand girl wants to come to Britain—and Europe. Britain's part of our heritage.' She glanced coldly at him. 'I don't know why I'm talking to you. Apart from being a bully, you're a friend of Sir Angus and his shooting cronies. You're probably as bad as they are.'

He shrugged. 'I'm a neutral. I met Moyra Deardon—Sir Angus's daughter—while she was touring the States. We became friendly and she invited me to stay with them if ever I came to Scotland. So here I am.'

She said shortly. 'I've heard of Moyra Deardon. She's the—the international model?'

He nodded. 'And an occasional actress. And a glamorous jet-setter,' he added.

'I expect you see a lot of her—living at the Castle?'

'No, I'm not in the Castle—through choice. Sir Angus let me have a little cottage in the Castle grounds. I've made a temporary darkroom there and I'm pretty self-contained.'

'What are you in Scotland for?'

'To cover some assignments. Highland Games, the Duntochter Festival, the Gathering of the Clans, trout fishing, the whisky industry—and the deer-hunting.'

Fiona sniffed. 'I think it would be repulsive, taking pictures of deer being shot.'

Gordon Ross grunted. 'It's not my idea of a fun job either, but a magazine I work for wants it covered. If it's any comfort, their editorial line is anti-blood sports. I've made this clear to Sir Angus, but he doesn't mind. Or anyway, Moyra tells him he mustn't mind, so he puts up with me—as well as putting me up.'

'I hope what you write gives both sides of the story.'

He nodded. 'Your side will get a fair run. I'd like to meet your friends—the ones with you today. Get their viewpoint.'

'I'll think about it,' she said as he slowed the Land Rover to negotiate a gully. Then as they climbed out of the gully she saw a dry stone dyke fringing a narrow gravel road. Gordon Ross followed the dyke until he came to a gate then got out and opened it and drove through then got out and closed the gate. Back behind the wheel, he changed into two-wheel drive, then started off along the gravel road.

'This will take us on to the main Duntochter road,' he said. 'Through the village, then past the Castle to your place. Is that right?'

Fiona nodded and shivered slightly.

He glanced at her. 'We better get you into some dry clothes, fast.'

He leaned over and closed the air vent on her side. Now that the vehicle was moving at speed the rush of air was cool on her sodden clothes. She shivered again and he increased speed until they came to a junction on to the bitumen road which the locals called the main road, although it was quite narrow. He reached Duntochter village and sped through its single main street, then began the upward climb towards the Castle.

He said, 'It's still a few miles to Elgin House. We're just coming to the Castle.'

On a rise to their right Fiona could see the ivy-covered towers and battlements of Duntochter Castle rearing its square granite mass over the surrounding fields grazed by shaggy Highland cattle with their wide horns.

The Castle stood about two miles off the road in heavily-wooded parkland, and as they approached its huge ornate iron gates in the surrounding wall, Gordon Ross said abruptly, 'I'm going to take you to my place and get you some dry clothes, then I'll run you home.'

Before she could protest, he swung the Land Rover off the road and through the open gates, past the gatekeeper's cottage where a gnarled old man in a tartan bonnet smoking a clay pipe raised a hand in acknowledgment.

'That's Wullie McNair,' Gordon said. 'He's been gatekeeper for years. I took some Polaroid pictures of him when I first got here and gave him them, and since then he's been my friend for life.'

Fiona shrugged uninterestedly as the Land Rover crunched along the red gravel drive which was bordered by dense plantings of beech, oak and sycamore. In the autumn sun the woods were a blaze of red, gold and russet. He said, 'Fall is sure a lovely time in Scotland. It reminds me of New England.'

She said, 'October is the most colourful month in the Highlands. I've borrowed Mrs Stewart's bicycle a few times and ridden along the paths over the moors. It's the best way to really see the Highlands.'

She shivered again and he increased speed slightly from the ten miles an hour he had been doing. He drove until he came to a rutted track that led off the drive. He drove carefully along the track for a few yards until a small whitewashed cottage with a thatched roof came into sight in a clearing.

Smoke curled lazily from the glazed brown chimney on the roof and Gordon Ross grunted as he stopped the vehicle near the front door. 'They're crazy about fires here. An old lady from the Castle comes down every day and cleans for me—and she always lights a fire. Whether it's rain or shine.'

He got out, then strode round and opened the car door and helped Fiona out. Then he took her elbow and steered her towards the cottage door which he pushed open. It was very low and he had to bend his head as he followed her inside.

As he had said, it was a small cottage, but inside it was cosy and pleasant. A wood fire burned in an open iron grate and on either side of the fire-place were two easy chairs, leather-covered and cracked with age, but soft and comfortable-looking. To one side of the room was an oak dresser with two glass doors behind which crockery hung.

There was a scrubbed wooden-topped kitchen table near the dresser, and two chairs.

Gordon Ross nodded towards a glass-panelled door and said, 'Through there is what's called the scullery. It's like a big cupboard, with a sink and a stove. Beyond it's a pantry that I use as a darkroom.'

On the other side of the room, let into the wall, was a large, recessed bed with a huge pillow that two people could have shared, and a big fluffy eiderdown. Fiona thought the big wide bed must be difficult to get at to make. Beside the bed was a wardrobe, and that completed the room's furnishings.

Gordon Ross closed the front door, then surveyed her dripping figure. His eyes glinted. 'Right,' he commanded, 'get your clothes off. Now!'

She stared at him, then she exploded, 'I will *not*!'

He sucked in his breath and stalked towards her as she backed away until she was stopped by the fireplace.

He said evenly, 'Yes, you will. If you don't, I'll strip you myself!'

She stared into his mocking grey eyes and her heart sank. He looked perfectly capable of carrying out his threat. Like a fool she had let him take her to this isolated cottage where she was completely at his mercy.

CHAPTER TWO

THERE was a big old-fashioned chiming clock on the mantelpiece and its ticking became unnaturally loud as Fiona stared at the craggy, determined face of the rugged American who had just issued her with an ultimatum. She moistened her dry lips, then said with forced bravado, 'I'll wait until you go out, thank you, before I get undressed.'

He shrugged. 'O.K. I'll find something for you to change into. Stand in front of the fire, warm yourself.'

He made no move to leave the room and she tossed her head and said pointedly, 'Well?'

He grinned. 'I've photographed models in every state of undress. Seeing you in your undies won't turn me into a raving sex maniac.'

He turned and strode towards the wardrobe, and Fiona picked up the poker and stirred the logs in the fireplace.

He came from the wardrobe holding a pair of jeans and a red lumberjack's shirt. 'The shirt shrank in the wash. But on you it shouldn't hang too close to the ground. You might have more trouble with the jeans.' He put the garments down on one of the easy chairs then grunted, 'O.K., so I'll go and unpack my gear. Oh, and you'll want a towel.' He went over to the dresser and brought

23

out a large fluffy white towel. 'There's no bathing facilities in the cottage,' he said, 'except for the sink in the scullery. I shower up at the castle.'

He tossed the towel on to the other easy chair, then nodded at her and went out the front door, ducking his head.

Fiona took a deep breath, then knelt and quickly removed her brogues and stockings, then unfastened her sodden skirt and stepped out of it. She pulled the damp sweater over her head and stood in her bra and panties before removing them both and standing naked in front of the fire. She glanced at the two small windows on either side of the door and thought their white muslin curtains didn't give much privacy from anyone who might want to peer inside.

She picked up the towel and began to rub her shapely body vigorously until it was pink and glowing. She did her hair in a knot on top of her head, then took the jeans and drew them on. He was right—they were miles too big for her, but she zipped them up and twisted the waistband into a knot almost under her breasts. If she was careful, and held them up with one hand, she'd manage to keep them on.

She pulled the red shirt over her head and it hung down almost to her knees. She buttoned it up, then sat down and rolled up the legs of the jeans so she could see her bare feet. She imagined she must look a weird sight.

There was a knock on the door and Gordon's voice called, 'Are you decent? Can I come in?'

Fiona called out yes and he kicked the door

open, his arms full of camera equipment. She stood up and clutched the pants as he surveyed her.

He laughed sardonically. 'What a sight!' he said. 'Do you think we should try and dry your clothes? You shouldn't go home looking like that.'

'I think I can,' she said shortly. 'I'll give you your pants and shirt when we get there.'

'Sit down,' he said, 'and dry your hair. I'll make some coffee—or is it tea you drink?'

She said coffee would be fine and he laid his camera gear on the bed, then went through to the scullery while Fiona unknotted her hair and began to towel it vigorously.

He was back within minutes with two steaming mugs of coffee and sugar and milk.

'I can't get used to having no ice box,' he said. 'And no shower. And no phone. Plus an outside toilet. But otherwise I'm very comfortable here. Although I'm glad there's electricity—else I couldn't have a darkroom.'

She said, 'Elgin House, where I'm living, is pretty modern. The people I'm staying with—the Stewarts—are very nice. They've made me feel part of the family—although there's only Charles and his mother.'

He asked about Charles and she told him how they had met when he had come to the B.B.C. in London to take part in a radio seminar on conservation. She told him that Charles was quite wealthy, his family had owned land in the district for centuries. But unlike many landowners,

Charles was not conservative in his views on many issues and he was often in opposition to Sir Angus and other landowners. She told him Charles was twenty-eight and his main occupation was managing the family estate.

Sitting in the easy chair facing her, Gordon said, 'You sound quite keen. You engaged to him or anything?'

She shook her head, colouring slightly. 'No. I mean—yes, I like him. But we're not engaged.'

He said, 'And what does Sir Angus think about Charles—and his friends—disrupting his deer-shooting? Don't they regard Charles as a kind of traitor to the landed gentry class—if that's the word?'

'Oh, yes. They don't like Charles. But Charles' family have been here much longer than Sir Angus. The Deardons are relative newcomers.'

Gordon sighed. 'That probably means only a hundred years or so?'

'Less than that. The original owners of Duntochter Castle were the MacPhersons—but the last Laird had to sell up. Sir Angus hasn't had the castle for more than ten years. But he's very wealthy, so he can afford its upkeep.'

He nodded. 'And how did you get tied up with the young radicals you were with today?'

'Oh, Charles and his friends aren't radicals. Far from it. They're really quite Conservative—but they're also Scottish Nationalists. They want to preserve the old Scots traditions.'

'I thought deer-hunting *was* an old Scottish tradition?'

She said earnestly, 'No—Charles says deer-*stalking* is the tradition. One man on his own, stalking the deer for hours. That's fair sport, he says. But deer-shooting like Sir Angus organises it is just murder. The gamekeepers drive the deer right on to the guns of Sir Angus and his friends and they just blaze away.'

'And that's what you and your friends stopped today?'

'Yes. We got between the gamekeepers and the guns and frightened the deer away. It was good fun,' she added. 'We had to crawl on our tummies for a long time to get into position without being spotted, otherwise the gamekeepers would have chased us away.'

Gordon studied her animated face, then said, 'You've really got your ancestral blood up, haven't you? I guess your folks were probably rebels in the old days.'

'My people weren't the rebels!' she said warmly. 'This was our country. My people followed Bonnie Prince Charlie—and suffered after his defeat.'

'But you're a New Zealander. How is this your fight?'

'New Zealanders are double-distilled British and there are more people of Scottish descent in New Zealand than anywhere outside Scotland. We're very proud of our Scots ancestry.'

He looked at her with an expression of slightly amused tolerance and she stopped suddenly and stared at him. 'I don't know why I'm talking to you so much,' she said. 'I should really be very angry with you—making me fall in the burn!'

He laughed. 'I didn't make you fall in the burn! You fell in all by yourself. And you made a nice mess of my cameras—although luckily you didn't break anything. Anyway, let's say we're square—or nearly. You could do one thing to make amends.'

Fiona choked. 'Amends? Me—why—oh——'

Her voice tailed off as she stared at his mocking face.

Gordon looked at her calmly. 'It's something you'd enjoy doing. And it could be quite profitable.'

She looked at him suspiciously. 'What is it?'

'I've got to go into Inverness to take some pictures, and I need a model for the foregrounds. A girl like you who looks Scottish. The schoolgirl type—attractive, but not sexy.' He glanced at her, enveloped in the shirt and baggy pants. 'Definitely not sexy,' he added.

'Thank you!' she snorted.

He shrugged. 'The shots are for the *National Geographic*. They don't go much on sex.' He added cajolingly, 'You get paid. How does a hundred dollars for the day grab you? And I'll throw in lunch.'

Fiona hesitated. 'I don't know. I——'

'If you could dress like you were today. A tartan skirt, and maybe one of those funny berets the Scots wear.'

'A tam o'shanter,' she said. 'Yes, I have one.'

'That would be very Scottish. And it would look good in colour with your red hair and green eyes.'

'I don't know if I want to get so—friendly with you,' she said stiffly. 'I haven't forgotten your behaviour today.'

'It could have been worse,' he grunted. 'I mean, I could have handed you over to Sir Angus, if I'd been a beast. He might have charged you with trespassing.'

'Hmm,' she said, glancing at him as she towelled her hair. 'Would you really have handed me over to Sir Angus?'

He shrugged. 'Maybe. Let's say your schoolgirl appearance saved you. I didn't want you to go to jail.' His eyes were expressionless as he looked at her.

Fiona turned her head away angrily and stared at the mantelpiece on which was a leather-framed colour photograph of an attractive-looking woman in her late twenties who held a little girl about three on one knee while a boy about six stood beside her. All three were smiling and the woman was blonde and beautiful. Fiona had noticed the photograph from the moment she came into the cottage, but she had avoided asking Gordon about it.

She controlled her annoyance at the way he teased her about her youthful looks and asked, elaborately casual, 'Is that your wife—and family?'

He shook his head. 'No, that's my sister—Joanne. And my niece and nephew. Their father's a Commander in the U.S. Navy. I take a lot of photos for Joanne to send him. She lives close by me and our folks.'

'Oh? The little boy looks rather like you.'

'Young Dustin? Yeah, there's a resemblance, I guess. It's the Ross family look. My descendants emigrated from Britain, too, but rather earlier than yours. Mine were with the Pilgrim Fathers.' He grinned. 'So I've got a Puritan background.'

Fiona glanced at his frank grey eyes which were regarding her with interest and her cheeks grew warm. Puritan? That was a laugh! The way he looked at her smacked more of carnal desire than puritanism.

She wondered if he was married, but decided not to ask him that on their first meeting. The pink on her cheeks deepened. She hadn't decided yet if there was going to be a second meeting.

He asked, 'And how about you? Do you have sisters, or brothers?'

She shook her head. 'No, I'm the only child. Dad's an architect in Invercargill and Mum was an air hostess before she got married.' She hesitated, then added, 'She was very beautiful when she was young. She nearly won the Miss New Zealand contest.'

Gordon grinned. 'So that's where you get your looks from. You might be very beautiful too, when you mature.'

She flounced indignantly. 'I wish you'd stop treating me as a—a child! I've had plenty of boyfriends, you know.'

This was quite true. She'd never lacked boyfriends. But she had found it hard to become serious about any of them. Boys around her own age had always seemed too immature, and often too full of themselves. She had never liked the way, especially at discos, the boys strutted around as if they were God's gift to women. She preferred older men, ones who were more serious—although not as serious as Charles. There should be a happy medium. She liked commanding men—so long as they had a sense of humour.

Gordon smiled, then said, 'Right—about tomorrow. I'm planning to leave around nine a.m. Think you can be ready—in your tam o'shanter?'

From outside there was a crunch of tyres on gravel and he got to his feet. Fiona said shortly, 'I'll think about it.'

He nodded as he strolled to the window and looked out. 'Ah, I have a visitor. Another female. This is my big day!' He opened the door and called out, 'Come in, Moyra.'

He stood back to let a tall, raven-haired woman in her late twenties walk gracefully into the small room.

Fiona had seen Moyra Deardon's photograph in magazines many times and also seen her on TV, but she thought she looked more strikingly beautiful in the flesh. Her jet black hair set off her high cheekbones that helped her photograph so well and her dark eyes were lustrous against her white skin. She was wearing a green and navy plaid skirt, knife-pleated, with a fuchsia shirt under a deep amethyst jacket of wool blend bouclé with a round collar. She had perfect legs and a good figure. Like Fiona, she wore brogues, but with light amethyst-coloured nylons rather than knee-length stockings.

She came into the room and looked disdainfully at Fiona in her outsize red shirt and bunched-up jeans. Under her cool scrutiny, Fiona felt like something the cat had dragged in.

Gordon said, 'Moyra Deardon—Fiona Cameron.' The two girls nodded to each other. Gordon added, 'Fiona is from New Zealand.'

Moyra said in beautifully-modulated tones, with only the merest trace of Scottish accent, 'Yes, you're staying with Jessie Stewart and Charles. I've heard about you.'

'And I've heard about you,' Fiona said shortly.

Moyra shrugged as if that came as no surprise to her.

Gordon enquired, 'And what brings you here, Moyra?'

She turned a dazzling smile on him. 'Well, I wondered what had happened to you after the shoot broke up—or was broken up. We went to look for you, but you'd taken off. Did you get involved with any of these stupid people who disrupted the shoot?'

He looked at her then at Fiona and shrugged. 'No, I got involved with a damsel who—fell in the burn.'

Moyra stared at Fiona. 'Oh, that's what happened to you?' She glanced at Fiona's skirt, sweater, panties and bra which Gordon had laid in front of the fire with her brogues and stockings to dry.

Fiona sat still and said nothing.

Moyra said to Gordon, 'Daddy was really mad

about the way those idiots spoiled his day. I mean, it's all so pointless—the deer have to be culled periodically or they wouldn't have enough to eat during winter. If Daddy and his guests didn't hunt them, then the gamekeepers would have to shoot so many anyway. Yet these fatheaded protesters persist in making such a fuss. I really think they're just publicity-seekers.' She turned to Fiona. 'And your host—Charles Stewart—is as bad as any of them. Daddy is sure he was among the idiots who stampeded the deer today. It's really too bad,' she pouted. She glanced speculatively at Fiona. 'You weren't among them, I suppose?'

Gordon said easily, 'No. She was walking and she fell in the burn—slipped off the stepping stones near where I was.'

Fiona got to her feet and clutched the jeans around herself. With as much dignity as she could muster in her scarecrow shirt and rolled-up pants, she said, 'As a matter of fact, I was with them. I—appreciate Mr Ross trying to cover up for me, but I'm not going to deny that I did something I'm proud of. I think the whole idea of the deer shoot is barbaric!'

Moyra raised her eyebrows and Gordon sighed.

Moyra exclaimed, 'Gordon, I'm surprised at you!'

Fiona snapped, 'You should be proud of him! Because he was chasing me—that's why I fell in the burn!'

Moyra smiled widely, 'Sorry, Gordon darling—

I misjudged you. Except you should have held her there. Daddy would have handed her over to the police—and her friends too if he'd caught them.'

Fiona snapped, 'I'm glad he didn't!' She clutched the jeans round her waist with one hand, then knelt and scooped up her clothes and shoes. 'I think it's time I left,' she said coldly.

Gordon said briefly, 'I'll run you home. And how about you, Moyra? Will I see you up at the castle?'

She nodded. 'We'll be having afternoon tea in half an hour.'

She glanced with distaste at Fiona as she padded past in her bare feet, clutching her damp clothes in one hand and holding up her pants with the other.

Moyra said, 'I'll see you there, Gordon—after you've disposed of this self-righteous young girl.'

Fiona strode out and Gordon and Moyra followed. The gravel hurt Fiona's bare feet. She stopped and pulled the wet bundle of clothes to her breast and said, 'Goodbye, Miss Deardon. I'm sorry you don't feel as concerned as we do about wild life.'

Moyra said scathingly, 'There's an old Scots saying—don't meddle in other people's affairs. You should try to practise that. And not trespass on private property.'

Fiona tossed her head and made to stride towards the Land Rover, but the gravel hurt her soles and she instead had to tiptoe gingerly, clutching her damp clothes.

Behind her, she heard Moyra's laugh, 'Really, Gordon, where do you find them? Such a gutter-snipe!'

Fiona stopped abruptly and turned and faced them. She clutched her wet clothes in one hand and let her knotted jeans go, then raised her other hand and pointed it at Moyra and took a deep breath preparatory to making an angry retort. The beautiful actress's brow darkened as she stared at the furious red-haired girl in her oversize male clothing.

Unfortunately for Fiona, she had no time to get any words out, for her jeans slid down over her hips and she dropped the bundle of clothes and grabbed with both hands at her falling pants. Quickly she hauled them up, her face flaming with humiliation.

Gordon raised his eyes and Moyra laughed loudly. He strode forward and picked up the fallen garments and said to Fiona, 'Maybe you should keep both hands for holding up your pants.'

He waved to Moyra, then took Fiona's arm and led her round and opened the passenger door for her, while she got in, still red and quivering with mortification.

He got in behind the wheel and started the Land Rover, then backed it down the narrow track towards the drive.

'You know,' he said conversationally, 'you re-alise that when you blush, you turn pink all over?'

Her colour deepened as she stared straight ahead. She said shortly, 'I made a mess of that. But she riled me!'

He nodded. 'I think she felt the same about you. I've never seen Moyra lose her cool before. I don't think you appeal to her.'

'I don't think I appeal to any of Moyra Deardon's friends,' Fiona said tersely.

Gordon glanced sideways at her. 'I don't know,' he murmured, 'you have a certain gamin, urchin-like appeal. Dressed or undressed.'

Her face flamed again as she clutched her wet clothes to her bosom.

He said calmly as they turned into the castle drive, 'So—I'll pick you up at nine tomorrow morning? O.K.?'

She looked straight ahead and said coldly, 'I certainly wouldn't depend on that. I may have plans for tomorrow.'

He leaned across and put one hand on her knee. 'Well,' he drawled, 'I have plans for tomorrow too. And they include having you as my model for the day.'

She tossed her head. 'You're very sure of yourself,' she said icily. 'And would you please remove your hand from my knee?'

He squeezed her knee before removing his hand and putting it on the gear shift.

Fiona sat in sullen silence as he turned the vehicle on to the main road. She thought she must have rocks in her head, even considering going with him tomorrow and posing for him. He was really a very unpleasant man, and he was so damned arrogant and self-assured. But, worst of all, he insisted on treating her as if she was a kid! At nineteen she felt she was very definitely a woman. At the B.B.C. some of the producers regarded her as mature for her age and Charles and his friends certainly treated her as a responsible—and concerned—adult, which she was, legally and every other way.

But because of the bizarre way she had met Gordon Ross—and the humiliations she had later suffered—he treated her like an unruly teenager. An urchin, he'd called her, and gamin—whatever that meant. It didn't sound complimentary.

She glanced at him covertly. His jaw was firmly set and he looked ahead and made no attempt to talk to her any more. As far as he was concerned, he had hired her for next day and that was that. She thought she would wait until she got out of the car at Elgin House, then she'd tell him to go to blazes and thumb her nose at him. But no, that would be childish, she'd better not do that. She'd just tell him quietly, and with dignity, that she didn't want to see him again, thank you.

Then she stole another glance at him. He did look rather—nice? No, that wasn't the word. Interesting, that was more like it. Very interesting, and even a little dangerous. With his determined chin and fair hair blowing in the wind he looked very like a Viking. She thought it might be—intriguing—to spend a day with him and be his model. She had never modelled before, so that would be something new. Then, too, a hundred dollars was about forty pounds. Good pay for standing around and being photographed.

When they reached Elgin House Gordon pulled up outside the front gate and said, 'Right, here we are. Make sure you're ready on time tomorrow.'

Fiona tossed her head as she slid out of the door. 'I'll think about it,' she said curtly.

He grunted. 'I'm not hiring you to think. Just to look wild, untamed and Scottish.'

She slammed the door, and clutching his pants and her damp clothes, strode towards the house.

She thought furiously that it would be satisfying to take him down a peg or two! But it might also be rather dangerous, for he didn't look the kind of man who could be fooled with. Anyway, she'd think about tomorrow and decide later. In the meantime he could stew and she would forget about him.

But in bed that night, she found it very difficult to put him out of her mind as she tossed and turned. His cold grey eyes kept appearing before her and she wondered if his expression ever softened and became tender. When directed at her, his eyes had mainly looked frosty, or else they had glinted with an aloof, superior humour. They had become tender once—but that had been when he looked fondly at Moyra Deardon.

She wondered what age he was. She knew he was over thirty, probably miles too old for her. To him she was just a kid—or worse, a guttersnipe—that was what the toffee-nosed Moyra had called her. Fiona flounced furiously in the dark, making the bed bounce. There was no way in the world Gordon Ross could be interested in her—as a woman. And yet, just once, when he had surveyed her in the cottage after he had commanded her to get her wet clothes off, she had detected—behind the gleam in his eyes—an expression that might vaguely be called interest. Or had it been lust?

She flushed all over. That was probably what it had been, pure animal desire. She turned on her side and hugged her pillow, turning it vertically alongside her body. She wondered what she would have done if he had carried out his threat and ripped off her wet clothes. A little shiver ran over her tense body. It would have been impossible to resist him—for long anyway. She had felt the strength of his powerful arms when he had picked her up and bundled her into the Land Rover. No, he would have been quite irresistible if he'd forced himself on her.

She thought it was a good thing Moyra Deardon had arrived when she did. Probably Moyra visited him regularly in his snug little cottage. Why shouldn't she? He was her guest as well as her father's. Fiona thought that was probably why he hadn't tried to force himself on her—in case Moyra dropped in, as she had.

She shivered again, recalling his craggy features and rugged physique. If she wanted to, she could see him again tomorrow. Her mind told her she was crazy to think of seeing him again. It could only lead to heartache. For how could she ever interest him compared with the glamorous Moyra? The best she could hope for was that he might treat her as a minor diversion—and she wasn't going to be party to that. No, phooey on him! She wouldn't go with him tomorrow—or ever see him again. She'd keep her mind clear and cool when she thought about him. That was relatively easy. The more difficult problem was to control the beating of her heart when she remembered his arms holding her.

'Brute!' she thought as she snuggled into her pillow. 'Who needs an arrogant bully like Gordon Ross?'

CHAPTER THREE

FIONA, in a light wool skirt of muted green MacKenzie tartan with red and silver checks, posed gracefully outside Mary Queen of Scots house in Bridge Street, Inverness, the historic capital of the Highlands.

More than one passerby stopped to admire the attractive, red-haired girl in her cream linen tie shirt which she wore under a burgundy velvet blazer as she posed at Gordon's direction to add human interest to the shot he was composing in the viewfinder of his Hasselblad. She had her nylon-clad legs gracefully astride, her blazer open and one hand on her hip while she studied a tourist map in her other hand.

'Hold it!' he commanded, and she froze into the pose until the shutter clicked, when he raised his head from the reflex viewfinder and nodded.

'Swell!' he said. 'I think you've earned lunch.'

Fiona relaxed her stance as Gordon joined her, scribbling in his notebook to identify the shot. He was wearing a soft wool blouson jacket with pleated olive cord pants, and the Hasselblad hung from a strap around his neck, as did a smaller Nikon. He was shooting colour on one camera and black and white on the other. He had left his heavy camera bag locked in the Land Rover which he had parked by the River Ness.

The photo he had taken was one of an endless series since they had arrived in Inverness at around ten o'clock. He hadn't used Fiona in all the pictures—'Having you in every shot would be too much,' he had told her. But he had posed her quite often, sometimes in long shots, sometimes in close up as they had gone round historic points of interest in the town.

In Church Street he had photographed Lady Drummuir's house, where Bonnie Prince Charlie had stayed before the failure of his Jacobite Rebellion and the defeat of the Clans by the English in 1746 at the Battle of Culloden.

They had gone to several other places and Fiona had found it very interesting, for it was only the second time she had been in Inverness. The first visit had been with Charles, but like many residents he saw nothing remarkable about the town's history and had only the sketchiest knowledge of it.

Gordon, on the other hand, had thoroughly researched the history of the region, and Fiona was slightly ashamed to admit that he knew more about it than she did.

Outside Mary Queen of Scots' house he finished scribbling his notes and said, 'This was never really Queen Mary's house. She visited Inverness in 1562 to show she was Queen of Scotland, but the Governor wouldn't let her enter the castle, so she stayed here. But he surrendered next day and was promptly hanged.'

She nodded. 'Scotland has had a bloody history.'

He glanced at her. 'I detect a definite lean and hungry look. You ready for lunch?'

'I'm starving,' she said, 'this modelling gives you an appetite.'

Gordon sighed. 'I've used hundreds of models over the years—most of them as skinny as rakes—but I've never known one who wasn't hungry all the time, and who couldn't put away gigantic meals.'

She smiled. 'I don't think I'm *that* hungry. But the Highland air makes one peckish.'

The weather wasn't as pleasant as yesterday. It was colder and the late Northern summer had temporarily vanished. Charles' mother, Jessie Stewart, assured Fiona that summer-like weather often continued well into October. Above their heads, heavy clouds threatened rain, and the sun came and went fitfully. But the light was clear and Gordon said it was ideal for colour work.

Before he had taken any what he called 'serious pictures', he had sat her on the bonnet of the Land Rover just after they arrived in Inverness. With the River Ness as a background he had taken several shots with a professional Polaroid camera. He had shot Fiona full length and close up, varying his angles and directing her to turn her head this way and that. After the colour photos developed themselves, he spread them on the bonnet and scrutinised them while she hung over his shoulder to see how she looked.

He grunted as he studied the shots. 'I was ninety per cent certain you'd be photogenic. But even the most experienced pro can never be sure—until he's done some tests. You're O.K.—good from any angle.'

She stood close to him as she looked at the shots and she thought they were the best pictures of herself she had ever seen. Gordon had only spent a few seconds on each shot, yet there was a striking difference in his professional product compared with the results from the amateur photographers who had mainly snapped her in the past.

She exclaimed, 'Gosh, I—they look terrific! I didn't know I could look so—so——'

'Attractive?'

She turned pink. 'Well—yes, I do—don't I? In the pictures anyway. You must be very good.'

He smiled. 'Being photogenic is a great asset. Some beautiful women just don't photograph well. Yet some of the world's most photogenic women would hardly attract a glance if you saw them in the street.'

He studied her as he collected the Polaroids together. 'You're one of the lucky ones. You look good in the flesh—and in pictures.'

She asked, 'Can I have these?'

Gordon nodded. 'Sure.' He handed her the pictures which she carefully put away in her bag.

Although their photo session was just beginning, she was already glad she had decided—after thinking about it all night—to accept his invitation to come to Inverness.

Charles hadn't been very pleased when she had told him during breakfast that she planned to go with Gordon to Inverness.

He looked down his slightly aristocratic nose and his pale blue eyes avoided hers as he sprinkled salt over the thick porridge his mother made every morning and which everybody, including guests, was expected to eat before they were served anything else.

'I thought you didn't like the man,' he said as he brushed sandy hair from his eyes, then added milk to his oatmeal. 'Last night you thought he was a brute—making you fall in the burn.'

'I've cooled down,' said Fiona as she surreptitiously sprinkled sugar over her porridge. Charles didn't approve of taking sugar with porridge and his mother approved even less. But Mrs Stewart was in the kitchen from where came the delectable aroma of kippers.

'I thought it was a good chance to see something of Inverness,' she said. 'You know—on a weekday when there aren't too many tourists around. You're always busy on weekdays, so I can't drag you away.'

He nodded reluctant agreement and she went on, 'I'll probably only stay until lunch time, then come straight back. I'd like to come to your highway meeting at teatime, and hear what you and Hamish and Colin and the others plan to do.'

His thin features became intense when she mentioned the highway. The highway project was part of the inevitable expansion of civilisation into the remoter parts of the Highlands. The region was split into two camps about the new project. The larger landowners, like Sir Angus, who lived in walled estates patrolled by gamekeepers, were in favour of it, as it would give faster access to the West Coast and its fishing. Others, like Charles, whose properties were already split by a minor public road, knew that motor traffic through their farmland would become heavier than ever once access was improved. Charles wanted to see the existing semi-wilderness retained and he believed increased tourist traffic would spell the end of its solitude and natural splendour.

He said, 'We'll be meeting about five and you can sit in. But this time—whatever protest we decide to stage—you are *not* going to take part!'

As Fiona opened her mouth to protest, Jessie Stewart bustled in from the kitchen. She was a plump, motherly woman in her fifties and had a round, freckled face and gingery hair well streaked with grey. She wore a large white apron over a blue dress and carried two earthenware dishes.

'He's quite right,' Charles' mother said firmly as she placed the dishes on the table. 'He should have his head examined for taking you out on Angus Deardon's estate yesterday. That was no place for a bonnie wee lassie!' She picked up two wooden spoons in one of the dishes and said, 'There's kippers or Finnan haddies to start with. Which would you prefer, Fiona?'

'Oh—I've had kippers before, but I've never had the haddock.'

Jessie carefully placed a large serving of the steamed fish on a plate and handed it to Fiona. 'And after that, there's ham and eggs and potato scones. Then oatcakes and marmalade, and if you're still hungry you can have——'

Fiona threw up her hands in protest. 'Mrs Stewart, I'll be fat as a pig if I say here much longer! I'm not used to breakfasts like this.'

'I know,' Jessie said grimly as she served a pair of kippers to her son. 'You told me. But we'll fatten you up before you go back to London.'

Yesterday, when Gordon had dropped Fiona off at Elgin House, Mrs Stewart had been full of concern when she came in dressed in Gordon's pants and shirt and carrying her soaking clothes. Fiona hadn't told her why she had got wet, only that she had fallen in the burn. Later, after Jessie had gone to bed, she had told Charles about it when they discussed the deer-shooting protest.

As soon as Fiona got in, Jessie rushed her up to the bathroom and ran a steaming bath and scented it heavily with pine bath salts. Then she had left her to soak while she bustled off and built up the living room fire into a roaring blaze.

After her bath, Fiona sat by the fire in her pink brushed wool dressing gown, glowing from the heat. Jessie came bustling in with a home-made concoction she had just whipped up. She stood over Fiona and almost held the glass to her lips while she swallowed the hot, potent medicine.

Fiona choked and spluttered, but managed to get it all down. Actually, she thought it didn't taste at all bad, although it had a pungent smell.

'What was in it?' she gasped.

'Ground ginger, cinnamon, sugar, hot water and——' Jessie hesitated.

'Go on,' Fiona prompted, 'there's something stronger, isn't there?'

Jessie looked slightly shamefaced. 'Yes,' she admitted. 'Some malt whisky. I don't like strong drink—but for medicinal purposes, I have to agree that it works.'

Fiona smiled. She knew Mrs Stewart regarded strong drink as an evil and didn't like having it in the house. But she kept a small bottle in the medicine cupboard, which she thought was the proper place for it. But Fiona knew Charles didn't share his mother's aversion to whisky. In fact, Fiona thought Charles drank too much, as did his friends, Hamish and Colin.

As Fiona finished the whisky-laden medicine Jessie told her, 'You'll never get a cold now, wait and see.'

Next morning, Fiona found she was right. She was up with the larks that sang all day around Elgin House and she felt as happy as they did. It was then she decided she would go with Gordon Ross to Inverness.

Charles knew about Gordon. He said he was quite a well-known international photo-journalist. But Charles was angry about how Gordon had treated Fiona.

'Although,' he said judiciously, 'we have to be fair. You could have damaged his valuable cameras. So I can understand him not being happy with you. You're a very impetuous girl, Fiona. You'll have to curb that.'

She had nodded meekly as he had lectured her. She thought his earnestness was one of Charles' less endearing traits. In fact, his tweedy friends, Hamish and Colin, were equally earnest even when they were drinking. Much as she supported their attitudes to conservation, Fiona wished they were a little less dull. She reminded herself that she was on holiday and wanted to enjoy her stay and see something of the country.

She was thinking along these lines as she left Mary Queen of Scots' house with Gordon and walked to the Caledonian Hotel. She felt absurdly happy at being with him.

She told him about Charles and his mother and what it was like living at Elgin House. She also told him about the highway protest they were planning, and he was interested but said he hoped she wasn't going to lie down in front of a bulldozer.

Fiona said she didn't plan to do anything so dramatic but implied that she was looking forward to some activity to break the monotony of the endless discussions Charles and his friends engaged in.

He glanced at her as they strolled towards the hotel. Her face was animated and glowing in the breeze and she looked as if she was enjoying herself.

He said, 'It sounds like living at Elgin House isn't a bundle of fun?'

Loyally, she defended her hosts. 'No—Mrs Stewart can be quite an amusing lady—and she's a very hospitable one. And Charles is all right, although maybe a bit—dour—you know that Scottish word?'

He nodded. 'Life at Duntochter Castle isn't a bundle of laughs either. But Sir Angus is also very hospitable. He loaned me the Land Rover, for example, and he can't do enough for me. But if it wasn't for Moyra it would be a dull stay. She puts some zip into the place and even makes her old man and his dreary huntin', shootin' and fishin' friends sparkle occasionally.'

Fiona imagined Moyra would add sparkle anywhere. Since she had met her yesterday she had recalled more about her and her well-publicised romance and marriage to a wealthy German baron a few years ago until she had divorced him and gone back to acting and modelling.

But she didn't want to talk about Moyra, so she quickly changed the subject as Gordon led her into the hotel. In the old-fashioned dining room they had cock-a-leekie soup, then freshly caught salmon, followed by roast pheasant, and Gordon watched with interest as Fiona ate every morsel, although she decided against any dessert.

'I had an enormous breakfast,' she said. 'I'm really going to be fat by the time I get back to London. I don't know why I eat so much up here. It must be the Highland air.'

He looked at her animated face, then he smiled and suddenly her heart seemed to turn over. His smile was totally unexpected, for he had been very serious all morning as he had concentrated on his work. Occasionally he had talked to her, mainly when he was posing her and telling her which way to look and how to look. He had also given her some historic background as they had moved around the town, but he hadn't been exactly loquacious.

But apparently he had decided it was time to engage his lovely young model in some light conversation, for he followed his smile by saying, 'I guess at your age you're always hungry.'

Fiona frowned. 'I'm nineteen, as I told you. You talk as if you were a million years older than me. What age are you?'

'I'm thirty-five,' he said. Then he added with a shrug, 'But I've been around.'

She asked him about himself, saying that Charles had said he was quite famous.

He admitted that he was reasonably well known and he told her about some of his assignments around the world he had covered for magazines. He described how he had started as a journalist in Boston, then branched into photography, to become one of America's top freelancers.

She toyed with her spoon, then said, 'I expect you've got a lot of girl-friends—all those models, like Moyra.'

Gordon smiled and she thought, two smiles! He really is starting to unbend.

Then he said lightly, 'I don't have many *girl*-friends. Not your age anyway. But I have a few women friends.'

I bet you do, she muttered under her breath. They're probably stashed away in every city in the world just panting for your call. She avoided asking if he was married or had been, and he didn't mention it.

He went on, 'I don't socialise much with models. Regrettably, what they say about them is mainly true—they can be pretty dumb. Especially the young ones. I think females have to reach twenty-six or so before you can have an intelligent conversation with them.'

Fiona knitted her brow as she stared down at her coffee cup and tried hard to think of something intelligent to say. But almost everything she thought of sounded inane, so she played it safe and asked what he intended to do for the rest of the day. Gordon told her he planned to visit Culloden Moor, a few miles out of Inverness, and take some pictures at the graves of the Clans. Fiona said she wanted to be back at Elgin House by five o'clock and he said they would do that comfortably.

At the Moor, on the site of the battle between Bonnie Prince Charlie's Highlanders and the English army led by the Duke of Cumberland, they had the bleak, windswept battlefield almost to themselves, and Gordon took a number of pictures of the historic site.

Then they drove back to Inverness where he stopped at a photographic shop and bought some black and white photographic paper. He said he shot mainly colour, but there was still a demand for black and white pictures and he developed and printed these on a portable enlarger in the temporary darkroom in his cottage.

He told her there was a traditional Scottish dance at Duntochter village that night and he planned to take some pictures there. Fiona said she knew about the dance and was going with Charles and a party of his friends.

Gordon said Moyra, Sir Angus and a group

from the Castle were going too. 'I guess it's a big social event in these parts. It's not exactly a swinging place, Duntochter.'

He dropped her off at Elgin House and said he would probably see her at the dance. Glowing from her day outdoors, Fiona went in to find Mrs Stewart at work in the kitchen baking a batch of scones. She asked Fiona how she had enjoyed her day and she said it had been very interesting.

Actually, she thought it had also been very frustrating. Mainly, Gordon had treated her like a kid sister—or somebody else's kid sister he had borrowed for the day and promised to look after. Once, he had even made joking reference to how they had met yesterday and called her a tomboy. She hadn't been called a tomboy since she was twelve.

He had been interested enough in her while posing her, but she thought he would have given exactly the same attention to a man in a kilt if he had been using one to add life to his pictures. His indifference to her as a female was really very annoying—and quite mortifying. At work, men of Gordon's age treated her as an equal, mentally and every other way. Socially she was always in demand and she never lacked dates. But this self-contained photographer seemed to think she was a juvenile not worth bothering about, except to add a splash of colour in his pictures.

Fiona decided she would see what happened at the dance tonight. Maybe then she would get the opportunity to make Gordon notice her as a woman.

Charles came home with Hamish and Colin and they gathered with Fiona round the living room table for afternoon tea.

Like Charles, Hamish and Colin were in their late twenties, and like him, they weren't married. They were both small farmers and mainly ran cattle, as Charles did. Their properties had been in their families for generations and they were well-known in the district.

Hamish was a bulky man with gingery hair and a large ginger moustache. Colin was wiry and thin-featured with black hair and black eyes to match. They had gone to school with Charles at Fettes College in Edinburgh. Sometimes they reminded Fiona of overgrown schoolboys, but they had strong social consciences and cared deeply about the Highlands.

Mrs Stewart brought in afternoon tea and Fiona thought the plates would never stop coming. There were four kinds of scones, pancakes, crumpets and a variety of jellies and jams, plus butter and cream and a big teapot that never seemed to run dry. Fiona thought afternoon tea was almost a meal in itself.

Mrs Stewart had tea with Fiona and the three men and they discussed local affairs and how their day had gone. Then Jessie bustled away to the kitchen when they began discussing the new highway and how they could register an effective protest against it.

Fiona knew the ceremony to mark the start of construction of the new highway was to be held on Friday at a small hotel near Duntochter. Sir

Angus Deardon was scheduled to unveil a commemorative stone. Charles estimated that they would be able to muster about thirty Scottish Nationalists to join the protest.

Hamish, who had some talent as an artist, was put in charge of preparing placards. Colin would handle transport to ensure that all the protesters reached the site of the ceremony. Fiona volunteered to help write placards and drive Mrs Stewart's car to pick up some protesters who didn't have transport.

'And that'll be enough for you,' Charles said dourly. 'We don't want you to get mixed up in any—disturbance—that might develop.'

Hamish said, 'I hear that MacGregor is getting some extra men from Inverness for the day. Sir Angus has pulled a few strings.'

Charles told Fiona that Sergeant MacGregor was the local police chief. They discussed various plans of action until after six o'clock when Fiona left them to have a bath and get dressed for the dance which was scheduled to start at seven-thirty.

Actually, during the latter part of their discussion, she had been thinking much more about the dance than about the highway protest. Then, as she lingered luxuriously in a hot, scented bath, she admitted it wasn't the dance that dominated her thoughts, but the fact that she would see Gordon again.

She smiled as she soaped herself. It was only two hours since he had brought her home and she had spent all day in his company—yet she was daydreaming about meeting him again.

Then her smile faded as she realised that tonight he would be with Moyra, so their opportunities of being alone would be limited. But still, at least they should be able to have a dance together, which would be something. The prospect of being in his arms made her already hot, pink body grow even warmer, and she jumped out of the bath and began towelling herself vigorously.

She would really have to stop thinking about him, she scolded herself. Or anyway, letting him dominate her thoughts. Moyra was much more glamorous—and much more available, being right at the Castle.

Fiona thought again about Moyra and her proximity to Gordon at his cottage. It was an ideal arrangement when they wanted to be alone and renew their old friendship, as Gordon had called it.

She avoided thinking about the nature of their relationship and towelled herself until her skin tingled. She glanced at her nude, curving figure in the steamy mirror, then discarded the towel and adopted a seductive model's pose and looked languorously at her reflection.

Then, suddenly selfconscious, she dropped the pose and turned on the cold tap in the washbasin and splashed cold water over her hot face.

Fiona, she told herself despondently, stop thinking about him. He regards you as a mere harum-scarum teenager. What makes you think you can compete with a beautiful woman like

Moyra—or all his other glamorous, jet-setting females?

She studied her dripping face in the mirror and frowned. For the first time in her life she had met a man who really interested her. Trust her to pick one who moved in a world that was right out of her orbit!

Then she thought dreamily, he was a man, wasn't he? Why couldn't he become interested in her? She certainly wasn't repulsive. The B.B.C. had even used her a few times in crowd scenes in TV productions. So she was attractive enough. Gordon had admitted that himself when he had taken her test pictures. Her problem was that he didn't regard her seriously as a woman. And that sprang from the bizarre way they had met, when she *had* behaved like a tomboy.

Well, tonight she would show him a new, mature Fiona. She would be very poised and ladylike and not get involved in anything juvenile. She might even try and be sexy, she thought, her face becoming pinker.

Then she poked out her tongue at her reflection and buried her hot face in the towel.

CHAPTER FOUR

THE Duntochter village dance was a fairly formal affair, and Charles told Fiona that everybody who was anybody in the district would be there.

He wore his dress kilt in the Royal Stewart tartan with a green velvet waistcoat, a white shirt and a black bow tie. On his feet he wore polished evening brogues and green knee-length stockings with a silver *skean dhu* tucked into the top of one stocking.

Fiona wore a long white dress with a demure neckline and a flowing pleated skirt. She added a shoulder sash in the red Cameron tartan and on the sash she pinned a large cairngorm—an amber-coloured stone set in a brooch. The brooch was a family heirloom loaned to her by Mrs Stewart. She let her red hair hang down her back and applied make-up sparingly. She knew that even these days, many Highlanders had an old-fashioned aversion to 'painted women'.

The dance was held at the Duntochter Church Hall, and when Fiona and Charles arrived in his two-seater MG they met Hamish and Colin and two girls, who had all come in Colin's Citroën. Hamish and Colin were very merry, as was Charles, and Fiona suspected he had been at his mother's medicinal Scotch in the bathroom cupboard or else he had a private supply in his bedroom.

They parked their cars in the narrow main street a few hundred yards from the Hall, and Fiona was introduced to the two girls, who, like her, were in long gowns with tartan sashes. Hamish and Colin, like Charles, were in dress kilt regalia, wearing the tartan of their clans.

As they entered the foyer, they saw that prominent among those milling around was the large fatherly figure of a police sergeant. He was in uniform, but hatless.

'Hello, MacGregor,' Charles said breezily. 'You here on duty?'

The ruddy-faced sergeant smiled, 'No, Mr Stewart. I'm here to sell raffle tickets for the police boys club. One of my more pleasant duties. And——' he lowered his voice, 'unofficially, of course, I'm the chucker-out as usual if anybody has a dram too much.'

Charles laughed as he introduced Fiona to the sergeant. She thought it was rather nice the way policemen in rural Scotland were very much part of the community.

Inside, the staid Church Hall had been transformed for the occasion with autumn flowers, bunting, balloons and decorations. Music was provided by a five-piece band, mainly fiddles, plus two bagpipers.

When Fiona and Charles entered, the dancing was in full swing and there were over a hundred people crowded into the small hall.

Most of the dances were old-time, like the Dashing White Sergeant, the Lancers, the Gay

Gordons and similar. There were also a number of reels—eightsomes and foursomes—and Fiona was in great demand, for she was quite accomplished at Scottish dancing, having done a lot of it in New Zealand.

There was a bar in one corner and long tables laid with a buffet supper. Charles, Hamish and Colin were frequent visitors to the bar and mainly they drank large glasses of whisky, served in the Scots way—neat with no water or ice. They insisted on buying champagne for Fiona and the other two girls who made up their table.

Just after nine o'clock the buffet supper was served and Fiona, Charles and the others were starting on their plates when Sir Angus Deardon and his party from the Castle made a grand entrance.

There were eight in the Castle party, including Sir Angus, Moyra and Gordon. All the men, except for Gordon, were wearing kilts. Gordon had settled for a dinner suit and black tie.

Moyra looked dazzling in a long pale blue off-the-shoulder dress that revealed its Paris origins in every line. She too wore a tartan shoulder sash and she was the centre of attention as she glided into the hall on her father's arm. Her fame as an actress, and her position as daughter of the Castle, guaranteed this attention. But even if she hadn't been a personality, she would have been outstanding for her beauty and sophisticated elegance.

Sir Angus was a big, heavily-built man, close to sixty, with a black beard in which there was no sign of grey. Fiona thought he looked splendid in his Highland regalia as she looked into his black eyes which narrowed as they swept the hall and surveyed everyone present.

His eyes alighted briefly on her, then on Charles and his friends, and Sir Angus scowled as he glanced at them. Then his party was ushered to a reserved table near the dance floor quite close to where Fiona was seated. Gordon glanced over towards Fiona as he held out a chair for Moyra and he nodded to her and she nodded back.

Sir Angus and his friends looked as though they had been drinking before their arrival and they made a loud and noisy group.

Charles wrinkled his nose in distaste as he glanced at them. 'Damned peasants,' he said, 'Classic *nouveau-riche*—taking over the Highlands.'

Gordon, after a few minutes, got up and strolled over to Fiona's table and gave a slight bow. She introduced him to Charles and the others and he shook hands with the three men.

Charles' manner to Gordon was distant. 'No camera, I see? Fiona said you intend taking some pictures of our little country dance.'

Gordon nodded. 'I have a camera outside in the Land Rover. I'll get it later.'

'I hope you're not going to be flashing lights in our eyes,' Charles said. 'Quite blinding, those things.'

Gordon shook his head. 'No, I'm planning to use available light. I'll be unobtrusive.'

Charles half-turned his back on Gordon and

began to talk to Colin's girl. Gordon said quietly to Fiona, 'I completely forgot to give you your modelling fee when we finished today. But I'll drop it in tomorrow.'

She smiled. 'I don't really want to be paid for today. I enjoyed myself.'

He shook his head. 'No, our relationship has got to be on a professional basis. I'll fix it tomorrow.'

Behind him, Fiona saw Moyra leave her table and she watched as she came over and stood beside Gordon. Charles, Hamish and Colin, who all knew her, stood up and they exchanged slightly forced pleasantries.

Moyra confined herself to a nod to Fiona, who nodded back.

Moyra took Gordon's arm possessively as the band struck up the *Blue Danube*. She said, 'An old-time waltz, darling. Think you can manage to whirl me around?'

Gordon inclined his head to Fiona, then led Moyra on to the floor. Fiona watched them, and she had to admit that Gordon's fair hair and rugged good looks were a perfect foil for Moyra's dark beauty. They made a striking couple. Too striking, she thought morosely as she watched them covertly, wishing desperately that it was she who was in Gordon's arms, gazing up into his searching grey eyes and feeling the pressure of his body against hers.

Charles and Hamish went off to the bar, saying they would get more champagne for the girls. But they stayed at the bar for a long time before coming back to the table with a bottle of champagne.

Charles' hand was unsteady as he poured the wine, and the band leader announced that the next dance would be a Ladies' Choice. Fiona asked him if he would like to dance, but he looked at her owlishly and said, his words slightly slurred, 'I think I'll—just sit for a while and—meditate.'

He raised the glass of whisky he had brought from the bar and took a swallow, then grinned at her. Beside him, Hamish looked equally under the weather. Fiona regarded them both coldly.

She frowned at them and turned her head away. She glanced across at Gordon's table and saw he was talking with two men. On the floor, she saw Moyra dancing with her father. The other women in Gordon's party had claimed partners and were dancing too.

She took a deep breath, then got up and walked across to Gordon's table. He rose and introduced her to the other two men, then she said brightly, 'Ladies' Choice—so I'm asking you for this dance.'

Gordon smiled and nodded to the two men and led her on to the floor.

As he took her in his arms he said, 'You rescued me from a boring conversation. Thanks.'

He danced well and Fiona was very conscious of his nearness as they glided round the floor.

'You're pretty good at this,' she said. 'You know all the steps.'

He smiled. 'I like touch dancing. It's more—friendly than disco.'

She murmured, 'Somehow I think disco would be out of place in Duntochter. I don't think they've even heard of it here.'

'No, it's quite a backwater. But I like it. I hope it stays like this and keeps its charm.'

'Not if the new highway goes through. The village will become just another busy tourist centre—choked with cars.'

As they danced, she told him about the protest planned for Friday, but she didn't give him any details. The fact that there was going to be a protest was common knowledge.

'I guess I'd better cover the ceremony,' Gordon said. 'This new highway and the controversy over it is part of the changing Highland scene.'

The music changed to a slow foxtrot and the bandleader dimmed the lights, and instinctively Fiona moved closer to Gordon. He hesitated for a second, then drew her close against his hard body and she let her head lie lightly on his chest.

They moved slowly together on the dimly-lit floor as the band played *I'm in the Mood for Love*. Little tremors of pleasure ran through her slim body as he held her close. He murmured, 'You're pretty good at this too. You fit against me very neatly.'

She looked up and saw a strange, half-quizzical look in his eyes, as if he was trying to adopt an amused expression but not succeeding. It was the first time she had seen him anything but totally self-possessed. She melted against him and felt his arm tighten around her. He let his cheek brush her hair, then she felt his body suddenly tauten and abruptly he drew away from her.

'Tell me more about Charles,' he said, his tone now brisk.

She stared up at him blankly. 'Charles?'

He nodded. 'Yes—your host. Who's getting very high.'

Fiona stammered, 'I—well—I don't——'

The music stopped and the lights came up as the dance ended. Gordon took his arms away and applauded briefly and the bandleader announced a break.

He took her by the elbow and said, 'I'll take you back to your table.'

She nodded, then as the applause from the dancers died down, she became aware of angry voices raised heatedly around Sir Angus's table. As Gordon led her from the floor she saw that Sir Angus was standing with two of his male guests having a heated argument with Charles, Hamish and Colin. Moyra was sitting in her chair near her father, her expression disdainful.

'And I won't stand any nonsense on Friday!' Sir Angus roared, shaking his fist at Charles, who was teetering on his heels, his face red and angry. 'I'll make sure MacGregor has enough police there to prevent you and your damned radicals from disrupting the ceremony!'

'You may get a surprise!' Charles snapped. 'Like you did at your deer slaughter!'

'I knew it was you and your radical friends!' Sir Angus shouted. 'You're damned lucky we didn't catch you!'

Fiona left Gordon and went to stand near

Charles. She took his arm and said quietly, 'Come away, Charles. It's not worth quarrelling with him.'

Sir Angus glared at her. 'And who are you?' he snapped.

Moyra rose from her chair and said sweetly, 'She's the girl from New Zealand who helped them disrupt the deer shoot. The one Gordon caught.'

'Humph!' Sir Angus snorted. 'Damn fool child! You should keep your nose out of other people's business.'

Gordon said evenly, 'I think Fiona's right, Sir Angus. This isn't the place to quarrel. Let's break it up.'

Two of his guests took Sir Angus by the arm and persuaded him to sit down, while Hamish and Colin prevailed on Charles to return to their table.

Fiona glanced helplessly at Gordon. 'It looks like we're on opposite sides!'

He nodded. 'We're sure in rival camps. I think I'd better get my camera and take some pictures before the dance becomes a brawl.'

Moyra took his arm and glanced coldly at Fiona. 'Come, darling,' she said. 'She and her friends are—quite impossible.'

Fiona's face flamed. 'At least I do care about—about the Highlands! And so should you!'

Gordon muttered, 'Ladies, we've just ended one argument. Don't let's start another.'

Moyra said smoothly, 'This is what happens when you come to a village dance. They let anyone in!'

'Yes,' Fiona said shortly, 'even someone as rude as your father!'

Moyra's lips tightened. 'At least my father and his friends are better behaved than yours! Look at them—completely drunk!'

Fiona glanced at her table where Charles, Hamish and Colin were standing, swaying slightly as they drank while casting lowering glances at Sir Angus.

Gordon said to Fiona, 'They do look pretty high. You'd better do the driving tonight. It would be safer.'

'Thank you,' Fiona retorted. 'I can look after myself.'

She turned on her heel as Moyra sat down and pulled Gordon down alongside her.

For Fiona, the night deteriorated rapidly after that, although the dance went ahead with a swing. She was vaguely aware of Gordon moving around the hall, unobtrusively shooting pictures with his Nikon, and she saw him take a shot of Sergeant MacGregor, who posed willingly with two attractive local girls in Highland dress.

But Charles, Hamish and Colin got steadily drunker, and the two girl friends of Hamish and Colin finally left in disgust and said they would get a lift home with some friends.

Fiona stayed with the three men, for she was determined to drive them home as soon as she could persuade them to leave.

But they didn't want to go, and Fiona became steadily more exasperated. 'It's after eleven,' she snapped, 'and none of you are capable of any more dancing. So I think we should go to Charles' place and have some strong black coffee while you all sober up. And I'll drive,' she added.

'We'll go,' Charles said imperiously. 'But I'm perfectly capable of driving, thank you.'

She tried to coax his car keys from him, but he wouldn't part with them. They were still arguing about it when they went through the foyer past Sergeant MacGregor, who had put his hat on to indicate that he was back on duty. The burly sergeant touched his cap as they passed and said, 'Goodnight, Mr Stewart. Take care there now.' To Fiona he smiled and said, 'Goodnight, miss. You look after the gentlemen.'

She nodded and forced a smile, and they went outside and along the street to where the MG and Citroën were parked.

'We're not going home yet,' Charles said stubbornly. 'We're going to Colin's place and we're going to—to plan our next move against Deardon.'

'You're drunk,' Fiona said coldly. 'You're all drunk. I'll drive you to Colin's place in his car. We can't all fit in yours.'

'No,' said Colin, teetering unsteadily, 'nobody drives my car.'

She stamped her foot. 'You're all crazy!' she cried. 'You'll get yourselves killed—and you might kill somebody else. You can't drive in your condition. I'm not going to let you!'

'How are you going to stop us?' Charles asked with bleary-eyed interest.

Desperately Fiona looked along the street for an ally, and sighed with relief when she saw Gordon strolling from the entrance of the hall swinging his camera from its strap. His bulk looked reassuring as he approached.

He stopped and nodded to the three men and Fiona. 'Hi,' he said, 'what's the problem?'

'They're too drunk to drive,' Fiona said shortly. 'I'm trying to persuade them to let me drive them all home, but they won't give me the keys.'

Gordon grunted. 'I think she's right. You should let her drive.'

Charles drew himself up. 'I suggest it's none of your business,' he said with dignity.

'Keeping death off the roads is everybody's business,' Gordon said curtly.

Behind Gordon, from the direction of the hall, Fiona saw Sergeant MacGregor ambling slowly towards them and they were silent as he approached.

He stopped and stood surveying them, rocking on his heels, his hands behind his back.

'Hello, Mr Stewart,' he said affably, 'I've been watching you and the gentlemen. Having a bit of an argument, are we?'

'No,' Charles said shortly, 'just deciding who's going to drive who.'

'I don't think any of you gentlemen should be thinking of driving,' MacGregor said judiciously. 'You had a fair skinful at the dance. I saw you have a bit of an argy-bargy with Sir Angus, but I didn't interfere—not in a social disagreement between gentlemen. But I'm on duty now and I—

advise—that you go and dig out Graham and his auld taxi and let him drive you all home.'

'I'll think about that,' Charles said haughtily.

'Aye, well, just be sure you don't get behind the wheel. In fact—I'll have your car keys, please, gentlemen. You can collect them at the police station in the morning. Come on, Mr Stewart— and the other gentleman—it's for your own good.'

Reluctantly, Charles and Colin handed over their keys. The sergeant looked at Gordon, 'Well, I know you're all right, sir. If you can take pictures like you were doing then you must be sober.'

Gordon nodded and the sergeant touched his cap and said, 'Well, away you go. Goodnight, all.' He turned and strolled back towards the hall.

Gordon said, 'I can run you all home if you like. My Land Rover's down the street.'

'We're going to Colin's place,' said Charles. 'We're going to have a discussion.'

'I'd rather go home,' Fiona said shortly.

'Then we'll take the taxi,' Charles said with dignity. 'Colin lives in the other direction.'

Gordon glanced at Fiona. 'O.K.,' he said, 'so I'll drive you home.'

'Thanks,' she said shortly, frowning at Charles.

Charles scowled. 'Yes, go with the sober Mr Ross. You spent all day with him—you might as well finish the night with him.'

Fiona's lips tightened. 'Goodnight, Charles. You're going to be very ashamed of yourself when I tell you about this in the morning.'

He laughed. 'We'll see who's ashamed of themselves in the morning. And I hope it's not you!'

She turned on her heel and walked quickly down the street. Gordon strolled after her and observed, 'Sergeant MacGregor sure keeps a tight rein on this burg.'

She said angrily, 'I'm really upset at Charles—behaving like that. I've never seen him so drunk before.'

He shrugged. 'It happens to everybody, some time.'

'It hasn't happened to me. I've never drunk too much.'

'Never?'

'No, never. I'm not that keen on alcohol. So it's not difficult.'

When they reached the Land Rover Gordon opened the passenger door and she gathered her long skirt in one hand as he helped her into the seat. The touch of his hand on her elbow caused a slight tremor to run through her body.

When he got in and they were driving through the village he said, 'I developed some of the black and white stuff I shot today. It looks pretty good.'

She cast a sidelong glance at him. 'Are they the pictures with me in them?'

He nodded. 'Some of them.'

'I'd like to see them some time.'

He glanced at her as he changed gear, then he shrugged. 'You can come back with me now and have a look. We pass the castle on the way to your place.'

'I'd like that,' she murmured.

'And I'll pay your fee while we're there,' he added.

Fiona smiled. 'So we can keep our—relationship—on a professional basis?'

He nodded. 'That's the best way to keep it. I never get involved with my models. It's a good rule.'

She forced herself to keep her voice light. 'And you've never broken that rule?'

He glanced at her, then said forcefully, 'No, never. And I've been tempted—by experts.'

In the semi-darkness she looked at his square, determined chin and began to hum to herself. She hummed for several minutes, then she stopped abruptly when she realised the tune was *I'm in the Mood for Love*.

CHAPTER FIVE

As she stood beside Gordon in the tiny darkroom in his cottage in the Castle grounds Fiona thought it would be difficult to find more intimate circumstances. Not, she reflected, that their closeness was affecting him, or if it was, he concealed it well as he worked briskly and efficiently at his task.

When they had reached the cottage and he had parked the Land Rover, they had gone inside where the fire gave out a welcoming warmth. Then he went to the darkroom and came back with two long strips of thirty-five-millimetre negatives attached to clips.

He told her he had developed the negatives when he got back in the late afternoon from their outing. The negatives had been drying while he had been at the dance.

'Then how can you tell I look good in them?' Fiona asked as he showed her the tiny negatives.

He shrugged. 'I can read negatives like other people read prints. I know they're good.'

'Oh,' she said, disappointed. She had thought she would see normal pictures, even small snapshots. But the tiny negatives were meaningless to her.

Gordon smiled. 'Cheer up! In a few minutes you can start looking at blow-ups of these. Come on, into the darkroom and I'll show you the simple mystery of photography.'

Fiona followed him through the tiny scullery, then into the big pantry he had converted into a temporary darkroom. On one side there was a shelf holding three stainless steel trays, each containing liquid. On a bench on the other side stood a small enlarger with boxes of photographic paper nearby. The tiny room was lit by an orange lamp which bathed everything in a subdued but clear light.

He pulled the door closed behind them and said, 'It was easy to make this into a darkroom, because it hasn't any windows.'

He switched on the enlarger, then slid one strip of negatives into the carrier. He exposed one on to the printing paper, then took the paper and squeezed past her and slid it into the first tray of liquid.

Using a pair of flat tongs, he moved the paper back and forward in the developer. 'Watch,' he said, and she bent her head closer to the tray. Gradually at first, then very quickly, the picture began to appear and she saw it was one of the shots he had taken at Culloden Moor with her in the foreground near the monument.

'It's fascinating,' she said. 'I've never seen photos being made.'

Gordon removed the print from the developer then slid it briefly into the next tray, then into the third where he left it to fix.

'I haven't any running water in here,' he said, 'so I have to wash the prints in the scullery sink.

I haven't got a glazer either for drying, but these are matt prints—which is the paper I bought today. So I can dry them without glazing.'

Fiona was leaning over the fixer tray, looking at the picture of herself. He had caught her at exactly the right moment, with her long hair and tartan skirt flying in the breeze and her face glowing and animated as she looked into the camera.

'Like it?' he asked as he slid the negative strip along the carrier in the enlarger.

'It's terrific!' she breathed. 'I—I'm amazed how—alive I look.'

His face was shadowed in the dim light as he said quietly, 'Yes—alive and—quite sexy, much to my surprise.'

She flushed and glanced covertly up at him, but he was concentrating on sliding the negatives through the enlarger. Gordon made about a dozen prints, skipping through the negatives and printing the ones where she was featured.

As they stood close together in the tiny room he suddenly grunted, then said, 'This is crazy! I've never processed film in a dinner jacket—with a companion in an evening gown. In fact, I've never had a girl in my darkroom before.'

'Oh,' she teased, 'and where do you usually have your girls?'

He glanced down at her. In the dim light his face was like a hawk's in the moonlight. He drawled, 'In bed—usually.'

In the orange dark room light Fiona hoped the pink on her face didn't show. He grinned as she moved a little away from his side. 'You asked for that,' he drawled.

She forced a light laugh, but for the life of her she couldn't think of a retort. She shivered slightly, but not from cold. If anything, it was warm in the tiny airless room. It was also very intimate in the soft light. As she had leaned over the print trays to look at the photos her body had frequently touched his.

Each time their thighs met she had had to control an electric quiver that threatened to make her knees buckle. She was glad she was wearing a long dress, so he couldn't see the trembling of her legs as she stood alongside him, her heart pounding and her throat dry at the proximity of his hard body whose masculine bulk seemed to fill the little room and make breathing difficult.

She wondered if he would take her in his arms and kiss her, or even put one arm round her as he stood close, his head lowered to study the prints so their cheeks were side by side and she was tantalisingly aware of the warmth of his skin and the pine-fresh male smell of his body.

But he gave no sign of being affected by their closeness and seemed absorbed in his work.

He said he wasn't trying to make the best possible prints, just rushing a few through so she could see them. 'If you wait until they're dry you can take them. They're yours.'

She thanked him, and he lifted the prints from the fixer and carried them through to the scullery, where he placed them in a large tray in the sink and turned on the tap to let the prints wash.

He looked at her for a long moment, then he suddenly cleared his throat.

'They'll need half an hour in the wash,' he said, 'then longer to dry. So let's have a drink. I haven't had one all night—I never drink when I'm working and I was envious of your hard-drinking friends—and Sir Angus and his buddies too.'

He led her into the living room where the fire still burned cosily in the grate. He tossed a few small logs into the fire and poked at them until they blazed.

He said, 'One of life's pleasures is sitting in fire-light. Since I got here I've done it a couple of times. All the lights out—and just the fire crackling away. It's the most relaxing thing in the world. A good atmosphere for contemplation,' he added.

'Do you sit all by yourself?' asked Fiona as he strolled over to the dresser.

He nodded. 'Yes—so far, all by myself.'

He picked up a bottle and said, 'Would you like Scotch?'

She shook her head. 'No, it's too strong for me. What else do you have?'

'Not much. Sherry—oh, yes, and home-made rowanberry wine. Old Wullie MacNair presented me with a bottle in return for taking the Polaroids of him. He persuaded me to try a glass and it's not bad. I don't think it's very alcoholic.'

She said she would try some and he poured a glass and brought it to her as she sat in one of the easy chairs. Then he poured himself a Scotch and went into the scullery to add some water.

When he came back he raised his glass and said,

'Cheers,' then he put his glass down and slipped off his dinner jacket and hung it over one of the straight-backed chairs by the table. He strolled over to the single lamp near the bed and clicked it off. The fire was blazing well and its dancing light illuminated the room. He picked up his glass and came over and sat in the easy chair facing her.

'Time for contemplation,' he said. 'What are you thinking about?'

'I'm thinking this wine is really quite good,' she said as she took her second sip. 'And what are you thinking?'

Gordon stretched his long legs comfortably towards the fire. 'I'm thinking how much like home this is.'

'In Boston? You have a place like this?'

He shook his head. 'No. I live in a modern apartment in Boston. But I have a cabin in Maine I get away to when I can. It's similar to this and in fall and winter I have a log fire burning all the time.'

Fiona sipped her wine and asked carefully, 'Does—do you share your cottage with anyone?'

He grinned. 'You mean a female?'

She coloured. 'Well, I meant a wife actually, or something.'

He smiled. 'No, I have no wife—or something. I work with an endless parade of women—mostly models—but I haven't got any special one. It's old-fashioned, I know, but I've always been married to my work.'

'And you travel a lot?'

He nodded. 'Too much. I'm reaching the settling-down stage. I'd like to get a place in the country—bigger than my cabin—and maybe put together a few picture books. And maybe raise a few kids.'

Her heart turned over at his casual addition about raising children. She tried to meet his eye, but she was flushing too much, so she kept her head down and sipped at her wine.

She mumbled, 'That sounds like a pretty good life.'

'Yes. I might make this my last overseas trip for a while. Have you ever been in America?'

Fiona shook her head and raised it as her colour gradually receded. 'No, I've only been to Australia—and Britain.'

'You'd like it in the north-east, where I live. Parts are similar to Scotland, and to New Zealand too, I guess.'

'I may get there one day,' she said, avoiding his eye.

Gordon put his glass down in the fireplace, then stood up. 'I'll go take the prints out of the wash and hang them to dry. Have some more wine if you want.'

He went through to the scullery, and she got up and walked over to the dresser and picked up Old Wullie's bottle of rowanberry wine. She decided she would have one more glass.

She poured it, then strolled over to the big wardrobe on the other side of the room and opened its doors. Among Gordon's clothes she found a spare hanger and she took it out and went across to the chair where he had placed his dinner jacket. She picked it up, then carefully slid it on to the hanger and carried it back to the wardrobe and placed it on the rail. She couldn't resist a peep into the low-set drawers on one side of the wardrobe and she saw that his socks, underwear, shirts and handkerchiefs were all stowed methodically.

She was smoothing the sleeve of his jacket when he came back from the scullery and he smiled, 'Tidy little housewife, aren't you?'

Fiona shrugged. 'My mother wouldn't agree with you. I was never very tidy at home, but since I started living by myself I seemed to get tidier suddenly. I don't know why.'

Gordon got his glass from the fireside, then poured himself another whisky as she closed the wardrobe. He went back to his chair by the fire and sat down and stretched himself.

She wandered over to the hearth and stood in front of the fire, which now blazed brightly behind her. She put her feet astride, then rubbed her bottom luxuriously, feeling the warmth of the fire on her rear.

'Hmm,' she murmured as she looked down at him, 'it feels good.'

He grinned suddenly and took a long pull on his glass, then said. 'It looks good too. Posed in front of the fire like that, I can see right through your dress.'

'Oh!' Quickly she drew her legs together, her face pink. She dropped gracefully to the rug and arranged herself, sitting sideways, leaning back on one arm.

She looked up at him and asked lightly, 'How did you manage to get away from Moyra tonight?'

He shrugged. 'She went to the dance with me in the Land Rover, but she had to stay and drive her old man back in his car. She thought he'd drunk too much to drive. Same as you felt about Charles.'

'Doesn't Sir Angus have a chauffeur?'

'Yes. But he likes driving himself. Dumb, isn't it? Mainly the chauffeur gets to clean the cars and service them. But when Moyra's home she likes to be driven, so the chauffeur gets some practice.'

Fiona fingered the amber cairngorm pinned to her tartan sash and he asked, 'Is that one of your family heirlooms?'

She shook her head. 'No, Jessie Stewart loaned it to me.'

He leaned forward. 'It looks very—unusual.'

She got up on her knees, then moved closer to him, unpinning the brooch as she did so. She knelt by his feet and handed him the brooch. 'It's two hundred years old,' she told him as he took it.

He examined it, holding it up to the firelight, and she put her elbows on his knee then rested her head on her hands as she watched him.

Absently he stroked her long red hair with one hand while he held the brooch in the other. A tremor ran through her body and he glanced at her. 'Cold?' he queried.

Fiona shook her head. 'No, nice and warm.'

He gazed at her as he stroked her hair. 'Your

eyes have gone very dark,' he muttered. 'They're not green at all now.'

'No,' she whispered, 'they're green. It's the firelight that makes them darker.'

He grunted. 'Your hair's still red—and it's very soft.'

'That's because I shampooed it tonight.'

Gordon reached for his glass on the hearth and abruptly drained it. 'I think I'll have another,' he muttered, drawing his knees in as he made to get up.

She put her hand round his glass and murmured, 'I'll get it for you.'

A shiver ran through her as their hands touched. Suddenly Gordon bent and cupped the back of her head in one hand and drew her face nearer his.

His voice was harsh as he said, 'You're a bewitching little urchin.'

Then his lips closed over hers and she let herself languish against his knees.

He fumbled with his other hand and put his glass down, then he drew her up on to his knee and his arms went round her. He pulled her tightly against himself and kissed her again—a deep lingering kiss that made her quiver with ecstasy.

He took his lips away and she laid her cheek against his chest and gave a long, shuddering sigh.

'Happy?' he asked, his voice low, his breathing uneven.

'Hmm,' she murmured, 'Very happy. It's been a lovely day—with a lovely ending.'

He grunted, then raised her face and kissed her again. When he took his lips away he was breathing very hard.

'You really are a witch,' he muttered. 'A crazy, red-haired witch.'

'I'm glad,' she said softly. 'I hope I've cast a spell on you.'

'You have!' he said brusquely. 'I said I never played around with my models.'

Fiona traced the line of his chin with one finger. 'But I'm not really your model. I mean, you haven't paid me yet. So our relationship isn't a professional one.'

Gordon slid one hand under her knee and began to lift her off his lap. 'Then I'd better pay you right now,' he said forcefully.

She clung to him, her arms round his neck. 'No—no! I don't want you to pay me. Modelling for you was just a—a love job.'

He grunted and slid his arms from under her knees. Then suddenly he smiled. 'I bet yesterday you never thought you'd say that!'

She tried to frown severely. 'No—not after the way you manhandled me, and made me fall in the burn—remember?'

Gordon grinned. 'I'll never forget it!'

She settled her head on his shoulder and murmured, 'Go on, admit it—you were a brute, weren't you?'

He nuzzled her hair. 'Yes, I'll admit it—if you'll admit it was your own fault.'

Fiona raised her head indignantly. 'It wasn't! You were thundering after me! I don't know what you might have done if you'd caught me.'

He grinned and kissed her. Then he murmured, 'So now you know. Although I thought you were the wildest, craziest girl I'd ever seen.'

'Oh? And you still think so?'

He smiled. 'Yes—but delightfully crazy.'

He kissed her again and Fiona lost all sense of time as his lips caressed her. Her arm, which had crept around his neck, pulled him closer and she was blazingly aware of the hardness of his body as she reclined on top of him.

He stopped kissing her for a moment, then told her, 'I'm planning to spend tomorrow around Loch Ness. You know, where the Monster is supposed to lurk. Want to come with me?'

She said dreamily, 'It won't make me very popular with Charles. But then he won't be very popular with me either, after the way he behaved tonight. So I think I can come with you.'

Gordon smiled. 'Right, I'll pick you up at nine. You can be my model again.'

'What do you want me to wear this time?'

'Anything colourful. Preferably something with red in it. But wear country shoes, I'm planning to do some walking in the hills behind the loch.'

'I'll wear my Scottish brogues, and a red sweater. How does that sound?'

'Pretty good,' he said, 'especially if you're not going to bother about a skirt. I could take some very sexy shots.'

Fiona ruffled his hair and he caught her arm and drew her down again and kissed her with mounting passion. She moaned softly as his hands gently stroked her back and his lips teased hers.

He took his lips away and murmured. 'I could stay like this all night. But I guess I'd better get you back to Mrs Stewart's.'

However, he made no attempt to move her from his lap and as he held her close she became burningly aware of his arousal.

She thought that for a man with Puritan ancestors, he was very sensual. She couldn't imagine him denying himself any of life's pleasures, especially the pleasure of female company. As he skilfully caressed her she realised breathlessly that this was no inexperienced young man who was making her tremble with rising passion. None of her boy-friends had *ever* made her feel like this. However ardent they had become, she had always remained in total control. But now it was different—and her state of disturbing yet heavenly turmoil was being expertly orchestrated by a man she barely knew.

She jerked herself back to reality and managed to remove her lips from his and rest her head on his shoulder and lie there, panting. She really knew very little about him, except that he was unmarried, but was considering settling down. She wondered if that was the truth. Or did he say that to every girl he wanted? She thought it was the kind of ploy a skilled seducer would use. He wasn't really a rake, just waiting for the right girl to settle down with.

But before Fiona could indicate that she wasn't going to be one of his conquests, he said abruptly, 'I could stay here like this all night. But, as I said, I'd better get you back to Mrs Stewart's. It must be long past bedtime, for a kid like you.'

He rose quickly to his feet and unceremoniously shoved her from his lap so she ended in a heap on the rug. She squealed in protest and glared up at him as he stood over her, smiling sardonically. She seethed with mortification. She had been about to tell him it was time they broke up the embrace, when suddenly he had forestalled her. Now he was looking coolly down on her, as if he had been in total control of himself all the time and had generously decided he wasn't going to take advantage of her arousal.

Fiona scrambled to her feet and glared at him, her eyes snapping. 'You're a pig!' she cried. 'You were *enjoying* kissing me! You were loving every minute of it!'

'Maybe,' he said, infuriatingly calm, 'but one of us has to maintain some self-control.'

'Oh?' Her momentary anger faded, but she was piqued. She'd see how much self-control he had! She stepped towards him.

'I'm warning you,' he said roughly. 'You're too—inexperienced to know what you're playing with.'

She moved closer until she was almost touching him. She moistened her lips. 'How do you know I'm—inexperienced?'

'By the way you kiss.'

'I kiss very well!' she exclaimed.

Gordon shook his head. 'You keep your mouth closed. You kiss like a—schoolgirl.' Her cheeks flamed as he added witheringly, 'And you taste like a schoolgirl. Kind of marzipan and dairy milk.'

'Oh!' She raised both hands to pummel his chest, but he caught them and gazed down at her flushed, seething face. Then suddenly he forced her arms wide apart and with one swift movement drew her against his body and kissed her hard, forcing the breath from her—and her lips open.

She panted against him until he released her, then stepped back. He grinned. 'But I like the way you taste, and how you kiss—or try to. If I gave you some tuition you could be very good.'

Fiona stared at him, her bosom heaving, then she said tauntingly, 'I know why you don't like kissing me.'

Gordon raised one eyebrow and murmured, 'Hmm?'

'Yes,' she said lightly, 'you're afraid you mightn't be able to—control yourself. Aren't you?'

He laughed sardonically, 'My dear child,' he retorted, 'I've had sexier females than you try their wiles on me.'

'That may be,' she said, triumph in her voice, 'but you're the one who keeps shoving me away. You're scared!'

He took a pace forward and grabbed her in his arms. 'O.K.,' he growled, 'you asked for it. Just don't start screaming when you get it!'

There was a light tap on the door and he frowned. He released her and glanced at the door. 'Who can that be at this hour?'

He crossed to the lamp and turned it on as

Fiona smoothed her dress and went and stood by the fireplace. Gordon strode to the door and opened it, and Wullie McNair stood there, tam o'shanter on his head, pipe in mouth and a long tartan scarf round his neck.

'Hello, Mr Ross,' he said, 'I'm sorry to bother ye at this hour, but Miss Moyra rang down to my gatehouse a wee while ago and asked if you'd got back yet. She'd just got home from the dance herself with Sir Angus and the rest of them.'

'Oh, yes. And what did you tell her?'

Wullie sucked his pipe, 'I said I didnae know for certain, but I'd walk up tae your cottage and find out if ye were in, then go back and give her a ring and tell her.'

The old Scotsman glanced past Gordon into the room at Fiona, and she smiled at him.

Gordon turned and nodded towards Fiona and said, 'This is Fiona Cameron, Wullie.'

Wullie nodded and touched a finger to his temple. 'Och aye, you're the wee lassie Mr Ross fetched home yesterday, all sopping wet. And then you went home wearing his breeks and shirt.'

Gordon grunted. 'You don't miss much, Wullie. I'm surprised you didn't see me drive past when I came back tonight.'

'Oh,' said Wullie, his face expressionless, 'sometimes it's best not to see *everything*. So what will I tell Miss Moyra, sir? Are you in or oot?'

'As a matter of fact, Wullie, I'm just going oot. I'm going to drive Miss Cameron home. So you could tell Miss Deardon that I came in and went out again—but you'll let her know when I get back.'

'Aye,' grunted Wullie, 'I'll do that now. They're having a party up at the Castle. They seem set for a late night.'

Gordon nodded. 'I may go up there when I get back.'

'Fine, sir,' said Wullie. 'And goodnight to you, miss. Now I'll get back to my gate.'

He raised a hand in salute, then shuffled off across the gravel.

Gordon closed the door and grunted. 'I think I've got a friend there. It's amazing how people appreciate a few free pictures.'

Fiona said shortly, 'If my free pictures are dry, I think I'd like to go home. I'm sure you'd prefer to go up to the Castle and join the party.'

He shrugged. 'I don't really want to, but I am their guest, so I guess I'd better put in an appearance.'

She nodded and forced a smile. Gordon glanced at her, then went through to the scullery and came back with a bundle of prints.

'Right,' he said, 'let's go.'

Outside the cottage, as they were getting into the Land Rover, there was a sharp explosive report from somewhere in the grounds of the estate between the cottage and the wall that surrounded it.

'Is that shooting?' she asked, startled. 'You mean they go shooting at nights?'

Gordon shook his head. 'Old Wullie tells me it's poachers—after Sir Angus's rabbits and other small game. But the shot probably came from the gamekeepers.'

'You mean they shoot at people?'

'No, I think they shoot over their heads.'

She shivered slightly. 'It's so—eighteenth-century—and so bloodthirsty!'

He nodded. 'Apparently the war between poachers and gamekeepers will never die in these parts.'

Driving to Elgin House, Fiona didn't say much. Finally Gordon broke the silence.

'About Moyra,' he said, 'the glamorous former Baroness von Ritter.'

'And what about her?' Fiona said brightly.

'Nothing—except that she's an old friend.'

'Oh yes. You met her when she was in America, didn't you?'

'Yes. I took some pictures of her, and she reckoned they were among the best she'd ever had taken. She wants me to take some more while I'm here. Actresses and models have an insatiable appetite for pictures, ones that show them looking glamorous.'

'I understand,' she said coolly.

Gordon grunted. 'I don't think you do.'

She shrugged. 'I don't know why you should bother telling me this.'

'I'd like you to know, that's all.'

Fiona said nothing as she thought about this, and Gordon didn't make any further conversation. She sat in silence until they reached Elgin House, when he brought the car to a halt outside the front gate. He got out and walked around to open her door, then gave her his hand as she got out. She stood looking up at him, then he grinned suddenly and bent his head and kissed her.

'Goodnight,' he said. 'I'll pick you up at nine. Red sweater, brogues—and skirt.'

He turned her towards the gate, then gave her a playful smack on the rump, and she moved forward sharply, then turned and glared at him. She drew herself up to her full five foot four then said coldly, 'I'm not sure if I really want to come with you tomorrow.'

He grinned, then raised one hand casually. 'Make sure you're ready on time. I want to take a lot of shots.' He waved briefly, then strode round to the driver's side and got in.

Fiona opened the gate as he drove off then she ran up the garden path. She thought he was really very infuriating. One minute he treated her like a desirable woman, then the next as if she was a child.

Marzipan and dairy milk kisses! Well! She supposed he meant she was very bland. Nothing spicy or interesting about her at all.

She let herself quietly in the front door and tiptoed up to her room. But she remembered the expression in Gordon's eyes after he had pushed her off his lap. He had been disturbed. Definitely disturbed.

As she undressed then got into her nightdress she hummed softly to herself. Yes, he had become aware of her as a woman, she was sure of that.

So, she mused as she went into the bathroom and did her teeth. What happened next?

If she provoked him again she might be very sorry. In fact, if Old Wullie hadn't interrupted him tonight heavens knows what might have happened! Fiona gave a delicious little shiver of mingled delight and trepidation. It was just as well Wullie had knocked on the door, or she could have been bundled into that big bed in the wall. And Gordon didn't look the type of man who would take no for an answer once he was aroused.

She shivered. She really was playing with fire, trying to provoke him. There was definitely no future in it, for at best he regarded her as a mere plaything. There was no place in his jet-setting life for someone as unsophisticated as her. How could she compete with the glamorous Moyra— and the dozens of other exciting women he met all the time?

She finished in the bathroom, then got into bed and buried her face in the pillow as she relived his kisses and his strong arms around her.

After a long time she drifted into sleep and dreamed she was back at school supping a huge plate of milk with marzipan floating in it.

CHAPTER SIX

PLAGUED by disturbing dreams, Fiona slept fitfully but woke early feeling surprisingly refreshed. Yesterday had been a long day—tramping all over Inverness with Gordon doing the photographs. Then there had been the dance at night, followed by the two rapturous hours in his cottage when he had kissed her and held her in his arms. Before she got out of bed she allowed herself ten minutes of delicious contemplation while she savoured the joy of awakening love.

She tried to pinpoint when she had first felt attracted to Gordon and concluded that it was while they were in Inverness. She thought it might have been when they had lunch, or perhaps while they were out on Culloden Moor.

Then she cast her mind farther back and realised that she had been interested in him since the first day they had met—after he had taken her to his cottage and given her his pants and shirt and made coffee. Even then, in spite of their unpromising start, she had found herself talking her head off and forgetting how arrogantly he had treated her only a short time before.

I must be a glutton for punishment, she thought wryly as she sprang out of bed at seven-thirty. She had fallen asleep thinking about Gordon and as soon as she awoke he filled her thoughts again.

She hugged herself, anticipating the hours to come when she would be with him all day.

She sang her way to the bathroom and Jessie Stewart called, 'You're in fine fettle this morning, Fiona. You must have enjoyed yourself at the dance last night.'

Fiona said she had, forgetting that it really hadn't been enjoyable at all, with Charles and his friends getting drunk. She wondered how he was feeling this morning.

At breakfast, Jessie told her about her son as she ladled a huge helping of porridge into Fiona's plate.

'He's not very bright this morning. And he won't get up—though it's long past his rising time. I've had a peep at him and from the state of his clothes and the sight of him, I'd say he was drinking last night and had a drop too much.'

She looked grimly at Fiona as she settled herself across the table and attacked her porridge.

Fiona said brightly, 'Oh, he wasn't too bad. All the men seem to drink at the dance. Sir Angus Deardon was there, and he was drinking all night.'

'Humph!' Jessie said sternly. 'I'll have a few words to say to Charles when he gets up.' She hesitated. 'And—he didn't bring you home last night. I heard you coming in then I heard him come in later, but he was a long time after you.'

'A friend drove me home,' Fiona explained. 'Charles went on for a—discussion at Colin's place.'

'Aye, I can imagine it. A boozing session, more

likely. And like a sensible lassie you came home with somebody sober.' She shook her head. 'I'll give him the sharp edge of my tongue when he gets up. He's a fair scunner!'

Fiona didn't know what scunner meant, but she imagined it was uncomplimentary.

Just after breakfast the phone rang and it was Hamish. Jessie told him her son wasn't out of bed yet, so he said he would talk to Fiona.

He sounded as if he had a very sore head, although with Mrs Stewart within earshot, Fiona made no mention of the dance. Neither did Hamish. Instead, he asked if she would like to come to his place that night and help with the placards for Friday's anti-highway demonstration. She said she would. Actually, she had forgotten all about the protest. It had got lost in her growing rapture as she thought about Gordon.

She dressed carefully in her red jersey-wool sweater and a green tartan skirt with fine sunray pleats. Looking out of the window she could see it was a lovely day, almost summery, so she decided she didn't need a coat or jacket.

When Gordon collected her at nine o'clock he too wore no jacket—just a red checked woollen shirt and cord pants. He cast a professional eye over her, then told her briefly that she looked very attractive. He held the door of the Land Rover while she slid into the seat, her feet in their stout Scottish brogues flashing gracefully as she tugged down her short skirt.

He got in and drove off, then remarked, 'You look like you slept well.'

She smiled. 'I did. And you—did you go to the party at the Castle?'

He nodded. 'I didn't have much choice. Wullie phoned Moyra and told her I was back. Then after a while she came down to the cottage and drove me up there.'

'Oh, and didn't she ask where you'd got to after the dance?'

He grunted. 'She was—a little curious. But I didn't tell her I'd been with—my radical Kiwi. That's what Sir Angus calls you, by the way. A kiwi is your national bird, isn't it?'

She nodded. 'New Zealanders are often called Kiwis. It's an unusual bird.'

Gordon grinned. 'That's a good description of you. An unusual bird.'

She glanced at him, but he averted his eyes.

From Duntochter, he turned off on to a minor road and drove across wild moor country and through secluded glens fringed by rocky hills clad with pines, firs and birch. Occasionally they crossed narrow stone Highland bridges, only wide enough for one vehicle. Underneath, brown burns burbled over white pebbles and moss-covered rocks.

There was very little traffic and they saw a lot of red deer. As they drove through a heavily-wooded section of road they could hear cuckoos calling even above the throb of the engine.

Near Drumnadrochit, they came on to the main road that fringed Loch Ness and drove south along the western side of the narrow, twenty-four-mile loch.

It was a beautiful sight with its grassy green banks and well-timbered hills rising behind. It looked entrancing in the sunshine and Fiona remarked that it didn't look at all like the grim and mysterious home of the legendary Loch Ness Monster.

They drove slowly along the lochside road, stopping occasionally while Gordon took pictures at some points of interest. As he'd done in Inverness, he posed her in some of the photos to add human interest to the shots.

As he posed her, she was aware of a marked difference in his behaviour compared with the previous day in Inverness. When he had posed her yesterday, he had touched her occasionally, perhaps to place her arm in the right position on her hip, or turn her head to the attitude he wanted. He had done it casually and professionally, as he must have done thousands of times with his models. Yesterday he had treated her impersonally, although quite familiarly.

But today he didn't touch her, directing her verbally instead. He made no mention of last night and avoided saying or doing anything remotely intimate. She was piqued; she thought he would at least say something.

They were standing by the parapet of a small stone bridge just off the main road. He had photographed her posed on the bridge with a background of an abandoned whisky distillery. Fiona leaned back against the parapet as he changed films.

She said, 'Don't you think you've taken enough pictures with me in them?'

He glanced at her as he snapped the camera back shut. 'Maybe I have,' he said briefly. 'I'm making a fundamental error—getting carried away by my model.'

'Oh! And why is that an error?'

She spread her arms on the stone parapet and leaned back and looked at him searchingly.

He let the camera dangle from its neckstrap, then siezed her and pulled her roughly into his arms and kissed her.

She melted against him—as closely as she could against his dangling camera. They embraced and kissed for a long time, oblivious of a horse and cart which rattled on to the bridge, a gnarled old Scotsman sitting in the driving seat holding the reins.

The driver cracked his whip as the horse plodded up the incline to the crest of the bridge. He ignored the embracing couple as his cart passed them. It was only when the cart rattled down the incline on the other side of the bridge that Fiona broke away and murmured, 'Did I hear something go past?'

Gordon breathed deeply as he held her. 'Just a horse and buggy. We've slipped back into a more—romantic age.'

'Hmm,' she whispered as she nuzzled his shoulder, 'I have a very old-fashioned feeling.'

He gripped her shoulders and held her out at arm's length. 'You don't look old-fashioned,' he muttered as he surveyed her curving figure in its sweater and short skirt. 'Very modern.'

Then he pushed his camera round to one side and drew her hard against his lean body and kissed her again.

Suddenly he released her and shoved her away. 'Right,' he said firmly, 'we've got work to do. Let's move on.'

He took her arm, almost brusquely, as if he wanted to show that he wasn't afraid of the physical contact. She let him lead her to the Land Rover and he held the door for her while she got in.

They drove south to Fort Augustus and Gordon kept the conversation on the region they were passing through.

'It's all very historic country,' he told her, 'steeped in legend—and romance.'

Fiona glanced at him covertly, studying the firm line of his jaw, his eyes hooded and his rugged face hawklike as he concentrated on driving.

'I know,' she murmured. 'The romance of the Highlands has always been in my blood.'

He shot her a quick sideways glance that made her heart thump alarmingly. Then he grinned and said conversationally, 'I'd say making love in the heather would be very romantic.'

He reached across and placed one hand lightly on her bare knee, and she jumped at the contact and her heart missed several beats. She stared at him, almost mesmerised, until he turned his head and gave her a long, lingering look. He murmured, 'Maybe we'll try it some time.'

Her throat was too dry for speech and her right

leg quivered from knee to ankle—and from knee to thigh—as his hand caressed her. She placed her hand over his and forced herself to lift his hand away, then she slid nearer the door and muttered, 'I suppose you've already done it.'

Gordon raised one eyebrow. 'Done what?'

'Made love in the heather.' She tried to keep her voice steady. 'With Moyra?'

He grinned. 'Not yet. But I guess Moyra isn't the love in the heather type. Definitely a boudoir type, I'd say.'

'Well, you should know!'

He grinned again. 'I should know about you too—but I don't. So far.'

On that threatening—or promising—note, he stopped talking as he concentrated on swinging the car round a series of tight bends.

Fiona glowed inwardly as she huddled against the door, shooting him occasional surreptitious glances. She was now sure that he felt something for her, but couldn't bring himself to admit it. Probably it disturbed him to find himself thinking about a young, unsophisticated girl whom he had first dismissed as a tomboy. Well, she was sure he didn't think of her as a tomboy any more—or even as a young girl. She was certain that in his eyes she'd very definitely become a woman. Which, she thought ruefully, created a new problem.

If she had become desirable in his eyes then he wasn't the type that was going to be content for long with kissing and caressing. No, he was a very—demanding type of male. Fiona had met demanding men before, but she had had no trouble resisting them, because she had never felt like this with any of the others. The problem with Gordon was that he only had to look at her to make her go weak at the knees. She guessed she would have to wait and see what happened. She was very much in his hands.

As they drove south she wondered uncertainly if she really wanted to become the kind of woman he obviously preferred. She still didn't know much about him. From that disturbing night in his cottage after the dance she had learned a little about what kind of man he was. But all she had really learned was that he was a very experienced lover. And he certainly knew how to provoke her interest. He had stayed almost constantly in her thoughts since they had met. She had a feeling that today might be D for Decision Day, and the occasional warm glances he gave her as they drove along only confirmed her premonition.

She thought she might have to call on all her will power to resist him, and she thought she had succeeded all right—if only she could control the fluttering of her heart when he touched her.

In Fort Augustus, at the southern end of Loch Ness, they lunched at a picturesque little inn. They had freshly-caught trout, but Fiona didn't eat much. Her normally healthy appetite seemed to have deserted her. She was too conscious of Gordon opposite her, their knees touching occasionally.

After lunch they walked through the little town and Fiona said she wanted to do some shopping, mainly for presents to send home to her folks in

New Zealand. She made a few purchases, then in a newsagent's shop she found a little volume of the poems of Robert Burns.

'I'm going to buy this for myself,' she said. 'I like Burns' poetry.'

Gordon shook his head. 'No, I'll buy it for you. A memento of your modelling days.'

Then he grinned as he plunged his hand into his pocket. 'That reminds me—I still haven't paid your modelling fee. It's two days now—two hundred bucks.'

'No,' she said, clutching the volume. 'The book will be enough.'

He pulled out some money and said, 'The labourer is worthy of his—or her—hire.'

'Hmm,' she said. 'Do you like poetry?'

'Mostly Walt Whitman's.'

As he paid for her Burns book she glanced over the books on the shelves and found a volume of Whitman's verse. In spite of his protest, she insisted on buying it for him. 'So you'll have a memento of your amateur model,' she explained.

He shook his head. 'You're very independent. I can't even buy you a present without getting one in return!'

In the Land Rover she placed their books in the parcel shelf and they drove back to Inverness, this time taking the road that ran near the eastern side of Loch Ness.

Past Loch Mhor he glanced through the windshield at the wintry sun. 'The light's just about right,' he said. 'I want to get one final atmospheric shot.'

He turned the car off the road on to a side track that followed a winding burn into deserted moorland. The burn narrowed to a babbling brook as they neared its source. There wasn't a soul around when he spotted a little plank bridge over the burn, which ran parallel to the track. A few wide-horned Highland cattle stared at them from across the water.

Gordon stopped the car and said, 'This looks like what I want.' He got out and studied the scene through the viewfinder of his camera. 'Fine,' he muttered. 'I've got all I need. Bridge in the foreground, cattle in the middle distance, hills and loch behind.' He grinned at Fiona as she slid from the car. 'I won't put you in this shot. I've taken enough with you in the foreground.'

A chilly wind was rising as he strode across the heather towards the bridge, and she watched as he began searching for the best angles, then took picture after picture of the scenic glen.

She took the books they had bought each other and went over and sat on a flat stone and began glancing through the Walt Whitman volume to see what kind of poetry he liked.

She was absorbed when she heard the click of a shutter and she glanced up as he lowered his camera and smiled. Gordon said, 'I'll call that Highland Lassie Browsing.'

He took the camera from around his neck and came and sat beside her on the wide rock. He picked up the Burns book and glanced through it, then grinned. 'Quite an earthy fellow, young Robert Burns.'

Fiona smiled. 'He did write *some* romantic poems.'

He nodded. 'So I believe. Anyway, thank you for your present.'

'And thank you for yours.'

She hesitated, aware of his nearness. Then she said, 'In the olden days, in Scottish marriage rites, the couple used to exchange books over running water.'

He glanced at her. 'True?'

She nodded, conscious of her cheeks becoming pink and rather regretting that she had started to tell him the tradition. 'Yes. Originally they used to exchange Bibles—but it could be other books.'

Gordon raised one eyebrow. 'And that meant they were married?'

'Well, betrothed anyway.'

He grinned, then jumped suddenly to his feet and seized her hand and pulled her up. 'Well, come on—we might never get a setting like this again.'

With one arm round her, and holding the Burns book, he hurried her towards the little bridge. It was only three planks of timber across the stream, which flowed rapidly underneath, eddying and swirling over white pebbles and small moss-covered rocks.

'I was only telling you about it,' Fiona protested, 'to show that I know some Scottish legend too. You've told me a lot of interesting things about the Highlands.'

Gordon smiled as he led her on to the bridge, then stopped in the middle and faced her.

'O.K.,' he said, 'what do we do now?'

'We—we just give each other the books.'

He nodded and handed her the Burns volume, then hesitantly she gave him the Whitman one.

He thanked her, then asked, 'And what's the significance of the running water?'

'Well, it signified the beginning of the couple's life together, and how they'd mingle and flow on and on—for ever.'

Her cheeks had become bright pink.

He grinned suddenly. 'And that's the whole ceremony? We're—betrothed?'

Fiona nodded and lowered her eyes. 'Silly, isn't it? I don't know why I told you about it.'

He drew her into his arms. 'I'm glad you did. But there must have been more to it. Like this——'

He drew her tightly to him and kissed her as the water babbled under the bridge below.

The wind rose and sighed across the moors, bending the purple heather and tugging at her skirt as she clung to him, feeling the warmth of his body against hers.

She gave a shuddering sigh as he held her, then she drew her lips away and gazed up at him. The amusement had left his eyes as he gazed back at her.

His voice was strained. He said, 'Let's continue with the ceremony.'

'That's all there is,' she whispered.

Gordon shook his head. 'That's only the beginning. Come on, let's get out of the wind.'

He led her from the bridge, then with one arm

tightly round her waist he walked her back to the Land Rover.

He kissed her, then opened the back door of the car and took out a grey blanket.

'What's this?' she queried.

He smiled. 'The continuation of the ceremony. You see, I know about the tradition too.'

'I think you're making this part up, aren't you?'

He kissed her nose. 'You've got to allow me some poetic licence.' Then he smiled, 'I carry the blanket to lie on when I'm doing nature pictures.'

'A likely story!' she scoffed, rubbing her cheek against his shoulder.

He held her arm while with his other hand he fished among the camera gear in the back and brought out a light brown windcheater. 'We'll take this too. To make a pillow for your head.'

Hand in hand, they strolled away from the vehicle until he found a thick patch of heather where he spread the blanket, then sat on it, drawing her down with him.

She was still holding the volume of Burns poetry and he took it and leafed through it with one hand while he held her with the other.

'Hmm,' he said, 'heavy on dialect, wasn't he, your Robert Burns? I'd need a translator to understand most of this. But no, here's some lines I can follow——'

He held her close as he recited from the book:

> *But for her sake this vow I make,*
> *And solemnly I swear it.*

*That while I own a single crown
She's welcome for to share it.*

He grinned, 'A Scottish version of "with all my worldly goods I thee endow". I think that's then followed by the bonnie bride promising to love, honour and obey.'

She protested, 'That's old-fashioned. Now it's cherish instead of obey.'

Gordon smiled. 'I still prefer obey.'

He let the book fall, then took her in his arms and kissed her as the wind soughed in the heather around them.

He nuzzled her, murmuring, 'Your nose is cold.' He placed the windcheater behind her then bunched it as a pillow. Gently he pressed her down, then ranged himself alongside her.

Fiona whispered, her throat dry, 'I only feel a little bit cold.'

He stroked her hair, spreading it in a red fan under her head. Then he murmured, 'I think I can warm you up—very quickly.'

She was quite sure he could as his hands caressed her skilfully, causing her slim body to arch convulsively as she strained against him.

He was really very practised, she thought sluggishly as her mind struggled to control her pounding heart. He murmured tender words in her ear as he kissed her gently and it would have been easy to abandon herself utterly to the heaven of his touch. But through a mist of throbbing arousal she was aware that none of the words he murmured revealed that he regarded her as anything but an intriguing challenge. Their romantic betrothal of a few minutes ago had, she was sure, been carefully designed to weaken her defences, as indeed it almost had. But for all his tender words, Gordon hadn't said anything that showed he felt more than mere desire for her.

She managed to draw her lips briefly from his and lay in his arms, panting, her eyes searching his.

'What's the matter?' he asked softly. 'Am I going too fast for you?'

She drew a deep breath. 'Yes,' she whispered, 'you are.'

He stroked her hair. 'All right, I'll slow down. I won't push you too hard. I'll let you—proceed at your own pace.'

'That won't be very fast,' she breathed.

He smiled down at her, his eyes mocking. 'You might surprise yourself,' he said confidently as his lips sealed hers before she could reply.

CHAPTER SEVEN

FIONA was deliriously happy as she whirled around Elgin House after Gordon dropped her there late in the afternoon on their return from Loch Ness. She was wearing his windcheater, which he had insisted she put on when the weather changed.

As she had lain with him on the blanket in the heather she had had no idea what the weather was doing. Most of the time, she had had only the vaguest idea what her lover was doing as he caressed her and transported her into a world of feverish rapture. It might have been snowing for all she knew as she lay in his arms and abandoned herself to his tender caresses.

But there was a difference between abandonment and total surrender, close as she came to giving in to his ardent wooing. While he tenderly aroused her dormant passions she was yearningly aware that he was a very experienced lover and that if she relaxed a fraction more he would possess her body as he had enslaved her mind.

She had to exert all her will power to break away and struggle into a sitting position and shakily hold him at arm's length.

Her skirt had ridden to her thighs and he stroked her knees and murmured, 'Your legs are cold—you must be freezing.'

She breathed deeply. 'No, I don't feel cold. You've been keeping me warm—as you said you would. Too warm,' she added, feeling her flushed cheek with one hand.

'All the same,' he said firmly, 'I don't want you catching a chill.' He lifted the bunched windcheater from behind her and shook it out. 'O.K., put this on. Then I'll rub your legs and warm you.'

He helped her on with the windcheater which hung to below her waist and reminded her of when she had worn his shirt the first day they had met.

He began to massage her legs vigorously, from her ankles to her thighs until her skin was pink and glowing instead of pale blue as it had been.

They kissed frequently and tenderly while he stroked her.

'You're very good at this,' she breathed. 'You must have helped a lot of girls to—get warm.'

He said solemnly, 'Not in Scotland. And never in the heather.' He reached down and caught one side of the blanket. 'We've been doing this wrong,' he said. 'We should wrap ourselves in the blanket, then you'd be warmer.'

Fiona caught his hand and stopped him pulling the blanket around them. 'No,' she said, 'I'm warm enough.'

He looked at her quizzically, then said lightly, 'I'm becoming very frustrated. Don't you want me to love you?'

She toyed with his ear lobe, 'Love me—or make love to me?' she whispered.

He raised one eyebrow. 'I gained the impression that you—wanted me.'

'I do,' she said, tugging her skirt over her knees. 'But I—I don't want you to think that I—I——' She shook herself impatiently. 'Oh, I don't know what I mean!'

Gordon said forcefully, 'We'll talk about it later. After I warm you properly.'

He began to pull her down on to the blanket, but she struggled and managed to stay sitting, clinging to him. 'No—no!' she cried. 'I—I'd rather talk.'

He looked at her, frowning. Then he gave her a little shake. 'You're a tease,' he said scornfully. 'You try to arouse me, then you back out.'

'I wasn't trying to arouse you!' she cried indignantly. 'Just because I wanted you to kiss me—and—notice me as a—a woman——' Her voice tailed off.

Gordon stared at her, then shook his head. 'Either you're a very cunning little witch, or else you're totally naïve. What do you think men are made of—iron?' He shook his head again, his face a mixture of emotions, most of them angry.

Fiona swept her hair from her face and said breathlessly, 'I'm sorry if I gave you the wrong impression. But I don't just give myself to a man—especially after only knowing him a few days.'

He stared at her, his expression sceptical, then he said sardonically, 'O.K., how long do I have to wait until you know me well enough to let me love you?'

'I don't know. It—depends.'

'Depends on what?'

She shrugged and looked away. 'If I think you—you're serious—about me.'

He took her chin in one hand and turned her head to face him. He said forcefully, 'I don't know what you mean by serious! But you've been one mighty distraction since I met you. I hadn't planned this little interlude, for example. I meant to spend the day working—that's what I'm in Scotland for.'

'I've been distracted too,' she muttered. 'I've—thought about you—a lot.'

She looked down and fiddled with the hem of her skirt, avoiding his searching eyes.

He shook his head, and then rain suddenly pattered against the steel top of the Land Rover nearby. Great drops splashed on them and he jumped to his feet and pulled her up, then grabbed the blanket. With his arm round her he hurried her to the shelter of the car. He bundled her in, then ran round and got in behind the wheel as the rain began pouring down heavily. He started the motor and the wipers, and looked at her as she sat huddled in his windcheater.

His brows knitted as he said, 'Tell me, have you known any man long enough to—give yourself to him?'

Fiona looked straight ahead through the wipers as they brushed the rain away. 'No,' she said, flushing.

Gordon moved over and took her in his arms. Then he forced her to turn her head and look at him. His voice was gentle as he said, 'I was right about you first time. You're not very—worldly, are you?'

'I'm worldly enough,' she said shortly.

He took a deep breath. 'O.K., you said it!' He switched off the ignition and flipped down the back of the front seat. 'Let's climb in the back. We can be very snug and comfortable.'

Fiona struggled in his grasp. 'No!' she cried. 'I'm not *that* worldly!'

Suddenly he roared with laughter and released her, then kissed her tenderly on the cheek. 'You silly little girl,' he murmured. 'You like to play with fire, don't you?'

'What do you mean?' she cried. Then she added indignantly, 'And I'm not a little girl!'

He slid back into the driving seat and re-started the engine. 'I'll leave it for now,' he said grimly. 'But don't try provoking me again. Next time I mightn't let you back out so easily!'

She opened her mouth to make a retort. Then she thought she'd better not. She *had* been playing with fire—she knew that. Remembering the strength of his arms around her, she knew that if he had wanted to he could have bundled her into the back of the vehicle and that would have been the end of her maidenly virtue. For that matter, he could have put an end to it on the blanket on the heather. She shivered slightly and clung to the grab rail as he steered the Land Rover along the rutted track.

When they were back on the main road he asked

conversationally, 'What are you doing tomorrow?'

Fiona smoothed her hair. 'I'm not sure.' She glanced at him. 'What are you planning to do?'

'I'm going to spend the day taking pictures at a whisky distillery, one of the oldest in Scotland. See how they make the intoxicating stuff that Scotsmen like to get drunk on.'

'Yes,' she agreed, thinking of Charles and his friends last night, 'they do drink a lot here.'

He nodded. 'It's the same in Scandinavia. It must be the cold climate. I've been in Stockholm and Oslo, and they drink a lot there too.'

She decided to continue with his non-personal conversation and said, 'Did you know that until the twelfth century, all of the Highlands belonged to Norway, in the Viking days?'

Gordon nodded.

She went on, glancing at his windswept hair, 'You have a Viking look about you—did you know that?'

He smiled wolfishly, 'Yes. And in the old days you'd have been a Scottish maiden and I'd have been a raiding Viking who abducted you from your village and carried you off to my home.'

'Humph!' she retorted, 'you wouldn't have found me easy to abduct. I would have fought.'

He glanced at her and half-smiled. Then he said quietly, 'When I'm ready—and if I want to—I'll abduct you. And you won't put up too much of a fight.'

She stared at him wide-eyed, and his grey eyes held hers briefly before he looked back at the road.

Fiona shivered inside his windcheater and hoped he didn't notice her trembling body. He was really very dangerous, and, feeling as she did, she should avoid being alone with him.

When they reached Elgin House he asked if she wanted to come with him again next day. He said he was committed for dinner at the Castle that night, but he hoped to get away early and process some film. Fiona told him she was also committed for the night as she had promised to help Hamish with the placards.

But in spite of her resolution of only a moment ago, she agreed to go with him on his photo trip tomorrow, which would make three days in a row she would have spent in his company.

When they reached Elgin House they sat in the Land Rover with the rain teeming down on the car roof. Gordon slid over and took her in his arms and kissed her.

'You're a distraction,' he muttered, stroking her hair. 'Moyra is going to be very annoyed with me, spending so much time with you.'

Fiona clung to him and murmured, 'Charles is going to be annoyed too.'

He smiled. 'Neither of us is being very fair to our hosts. We'll have to stop meeting like this.' Then he added, 'Pick you up at nine tomorrow.'

He kissed her again, then held her door open and she slid from the seat and dashed up the path to the house.

It was only when she got inside that she realised she was still wearing his bulky windcheater. She hugged it to her body and clutching the book of

Burns poetry, whirled into the kitchen where Jessie Stewart was once again baking scones for afternoon tea.

Mrs Stewart glanced at her glowing face and from her look, Fiona knew Charles' mother was aware she was in love. Jessie also knew it wasn't her son Fiona was in love with, and there was a trace of barely-concealed regret in her expression. She liked Fiona and she had had hopes that something more than friendship might have developed between her son and the attractive New Zealand girl.

But she only said, 'It'll just be you and me for tea today. Charles is out doing some work, trying to catch up. As well he might, after not getting up until late.' She pursed her lips. 'I gave him a piece of my mind, I don't mind telling you. It'll be a long time before he—he behaves like he did last night.'

Fiona murmured something placatory and Jessie sniffed, 'Anyway, he can get his own dinner. It's my women's meeting tonight and I'm going out.'

Fiona said she thought she and Charles might be going to Hamish's place for the evening and Jessie sniffed again. 'Aye, they're planning to do something at the ceremony for the new road on Friday. I just hope he's got the good sense not to let you get mixed up in their daft schemes.'

Fiona murmured that she wouldn't be doing much, then Jessie shooed her into the living room to have afternoon tea.

Later, in her bedroom, Fiona whirled around

for several minutes hugging herself in Gordon's windcheater, not wanting to take it off. Then she threw herself down on the bed and stared at the ceiling, re-living every moment of her day.

She knew now that she was in love, and, although he hadn't said so, she was sure Gordon felt something for her, though what it was she wasn't sure. A distraction, he had called her. Well, that wasn't entirely complimentary, but at least he was thinking about her—even when he didn't want to! Which was a good start. She knew exactly what he meant by being distracted, for thoughts of him had absorbed her virtually from the moment they had met. She found it almost impossible to think about anything else and every moment she wasn't in his company seemed a moment wasted.

She felt sure he must feel something for her. Otherwise why should he spend two whole days in her company—and another one tomorrow? It wasn't Moyra he was taking on his photographic trips, although she would have been a much better model than Fiona—certainly more professional. But then perhaps that wasn't what he wanted. Maybe he was using her because he wanted a fresh new face. Then she thought soberly that perhaps that was also why he wanted her physically—someone fresh and unspoiled as a change from the experienced women he usually mixed with. Her mind shied from saying women he usually made love with.

She sighed as she recalled the day and wondered what she used to think about before she met Gordon. Then she reflected that if she hadn't gone on the deer-shooting protest she might never have met him. But that was too awful to contemplate, so she thrust it from her mind and instead took out the volume of Burns' poetry she had placed in the windcheater pocket.

She leafed through the book, seeking the lines Gordon had quoted as they lay in the heather.

She found the passage, then began to giggle helplessly. For the lines were from *The Fornicator*, one of the very bawdy poems Burns was famous for. The four lines Gordon had quoted were practically the only non-ribald lines in the poem and were typical of the tender and romantic side of the Scottish bard and philosopher.

The rest of the poem told of one of Burns' many passionate affairs with a girl, Betty Paton, for which he later had to do public penance in the kirk, or church. He had certainly been a gay deceiver, Fiona thought as she read the ballad, her cheeks warming at Burns' frank verse.

Still, she thought, the lines Gordon had selected were very tender. She couldn't imagine him ever stooping to deceiving a girl.

Her reverie was interrupted by Charles' homecoming, and he banged on her door as he passed on the way to his bedroom.

When she met him in the living room he was subdued but half defiant, as if he expected her to chastise him for his behaviour last night. But she didn't mention it. She thought he had already had enough from his mother.

Mrs Stewart had left in her little car for her meeting and Charles said he and Fiona could probably get a meal at Hamish's place, as Hamish had a good housekeeper who did his cooking and looked after him.

They drove there in Charles' MG. Colin also arrived and they had supper before starting on the placards for the protest on Friday, which was the day after tomorrow.

They finished the placards about nine o'clock, when Colin suggested they all went down to the village pub. But Fiona said she was too tired and would prefer to go home. Actually she was too full of thoughts about Gordon and she wanted to be alone to daydream about her love. Charles said he would run her back to Elgin House, then, if she didn't mind, he would go into the village and join the others at the pub.

She said she didn't mind, although she couldn't resist giving him a warning frown before he drove off after dropping her at Elgin House.

'Now remember,' she said, 'if you drink too much tonight, then don't drive home.'

He said he wouldn't be late, as he planned to be back before his mother returned some time around ten o'clock.

After he had gone, Fiona wandered around the house, dreaming about Gordon. She strolled into Mrs Stewart's spotless kitchen and picked up various appliances and stroked them. She decided that she would like to have a kitchen like this, a homely one, where she could bake scones for Gordon—and, in time, their children.

Her stomach turned liquid at the thought of having Gordon's babies and she had to sit down. She hoped he wanted children. Then she shook herself vigorously. She didn't even know if he loved her—yet here she was thinking of them as husband and wife!

She ran up to her bedroom and put on his windcheater, which she tactfully hadn't worn when she had gone to Hamish's place with Charles. She stroked the garment, then thought, I could return this to him—tonight.

She desperately wanted to see him again. Earlier, when they had been discussing their commitments for the evening, and Gordon had been holding her, it hadn't seemed too difficult to forgo him for one night. But now, without him beside her, she longed to be with him—even if only briefly.

She glanced at her watch. It was nine-thirty. She didn't have a car available, as Mrs Stewart had taken her own and Charles had the MG. But there was Mrs Stewart's bike, and the Castle was only a couple of miles away. She could be there within half an hour, by which time it would be ten o'clock and Gordon should be through with his dinner party at the Castle and back in his cottage.

Even if he wasn't, she could wait for him there, because he never locked the door.

She knew he wouldn't mind if she was waiting to welcome him with a kiss. She promised herself faithfully that that was all it would be. Just a kiss—or maybe more than one. Perhaps a cup of coffee before she left and let him get on with his work. She sprang up and went outside and got Mrs Stewart's bicycle from its shed, then pedalled off through the dusk towards the Castle.

She thought as she cycled along, humming to herself, that in London she would never have dreamed of cycling alone after dark. Nor would she have dreamed of doing it in Auckland. But in her home town, near Invercargill, she would. That was the difference about country areas. A girl could feel safe on her own at night.

At the Castle gates she pedalled silently past the gatekeeper's cottage, but saw no sign of old Wullie. If he did see her from behind his curtains he didn't challenge her, for he knew she was a friend of Gordon's.

She pedalled quietly up the dark drive until she reached the wooded track that led to Gordon's cottage. Then, as she neared the cottage, she saw there was a blaze of clear white light spilling from the windows. She thought that was good, he was home. And he must be doing something photographic.

She dismounted and leaned the bike against a tree then walked up to the cottage. Before she knocked on the door, curiosity drew her to the lighted window and she looked in. Her heart almost stopped as she stared through the filmy curtains, and suddenly her whole word seemed to collapse.

The bright light came from two portable flood-lights clipped to the ceiling beams. They illuminated a small, cushioned stool, which was empty.

Standing beside the stool, wearing a seductive wisp of gauze around her lovely breasts and a long skirt with a thigh-high slit that displayed her slender legs, was Moyra. She had her arms round Gordon and they were locked in an embrace.

Fiona gave a strangled cry and backed away, then stumbled across the gravel and mounted her bicycle. She pedalled blindly down the track, tears stinging her eyes so she could barely see where she was going.

Not that she cared much. The delicate web of dreams she had been gradually weaving had been blown away by one gust of harsh reality. She wanted to keep pedalling on and on and leave the Highlands far behind and never see him again— or let him know how he had broken her heart.

CHAPTER EIGHT

NEXT morning, Fiona stayed in bed late. Nobody could say she slept late, since she hardly slept at all. It was only towards dawn, when the larks started singing in the trees, that she finally dropped into an uneasy, fitful doze, lying on her stomach, her head buried miserably in the pillow.

But haunting dreams disturbed even that brief slumber. Over and over again she saw vivid scenes of Gordon and Moyra writhing together in passionate ecstasy. She saw Moyra's bosom covered by a gauzy wisp of material which he easily ripped away before burying himself hungrily in her beauty.

She tossed and turned all through the night, trying to banish the floodlit scene from her mind—and the intimate scenes which no doubt followed her reeling, anguished departure. So that was the kind of photographic session he had planned with Moyra! It was simply a prelude to seduction, she thought, quivering with disgust. If she hadn't found him with Moyra, she wondered how long it would have been before he would have invited her for a similar session! All his protestations about his professional attitude towards his models were false, she thought bitterly. As false as he was. As fraudulent as he had been with her when he had used her as his model for two days while he coldly planned to take advantage of her love for him.

She shuddered as she recalled how close she had come to giving herself to him on the heather. She flushed as she remembered the intimacies she had permitted him and how abandoned she had been in his arms. Thank God she hadn't permitted him the final intimacy! Her guardian angel must have been watching over her as she lay with him yesterday on his blanket. The blanket he carried for nature pictures, he'd claimed. Huh! What a well-prepared, calculating seducer he was!

She thought ahead to what might have happened today—their third day together—if she hadn't found him with Moyra last night. She wondered if she could have resisted him—or would have wanted to. No doubt he had planned their third day together as the climatic one. In more ways than one, she thought bitterly.

She grew hot thinking of how stupidly naïve she had been. Of course Gordon had been having an affair with Moyra all the time. That was why he had arranged to stay at the cottage instead of at the Castle. They could hardly have shared a room at the Castle, with her father, guests and servants around. But how convenient it had been for him to have the cottage. So she could slip down there and be alone with him whenever they felt like it.

And she—provincial little fool—had actually believed he felt something for her! Oh, Fiona, she cried, after you'd given yourself to him he would have gone back to America—and that would have been the last you'd have seen of him! Women like Moyra made up his world. Glamorous, sophisticated women like she saw in magazines and in movies and on TV. Why on earth would he want any serious relationship with a girl who was still trying to adjust to cosmopolitan London after a backwater existence in New Zealand?

She really had deluded herself, she thought bleakly. Because they had met in rustic surroundings like Duntochter, where she felt at home, she had forgotten that Gordon's natural environment was the glamorous world of international jet-setters. So he had amused himself, planning to seduce her, relishing her innocence—and her naïve arousal—after the experienced women he normally played around with.

And boy, had she been innocent! Even that poem he had read—he had picked the only romantic lines in it to impress her with his tenderness.

She switched on the bedside lamp, then got out of bed and went over to the window where she had hurled the book of Burns poems when she had returned to her room after her flight from the Castle on the bicycle.

She found the page and stared at the poem again. *The Fornicator*—wasn't that apt. And at first she had thought it amusing! Some joke! But it was a joke on her.

Back in bed she tossed and turned until uneasy sleep overtook her. Before she dropped off, she decided dully that she would leave Duntochter as soon as she could. She would tell Charles and Mrs Stewart today. Then she would leave on Friday—if she could get on a train to London.

At eight in the morning, Jessie Stewart tapped lightly on Fiona's door, then peered in when she heard her stirring.

'Are you awake, dear?' Jessie called softly. 'I was wondering if you were all right, as you're usually up with the larks. I missed our wee morning chat and cup of tea.'

Fiona struggled up in bed. 'Yes, I'm all right,' she said woozily. 'I—I must have overslept.'

'Och, then have a lie in bed,' said Jessie. 'I won't bother you. But I'm going out in a wee while to do the week's shopping. So I'll leave a few things on the hob for your breakfast and you can get up and have something whenever you want.'

'Thanks,' Fiona said blearily, 'but I don't feel like anything this morning.'

'Och, you've got to eat something, lassie. I'll leave plenty for you. Charles has gone off to his work already, so you'll have the house to yourself. So take your time.'

Fiona got up shortly afterwards and brushed her teeth and showered. Then she pulled on her pink brushed wool robe and went downstairs. She didn't feel like dressing, apart from not feeling like eating.

In the kitchen, she made herself a cup of coffee, looking wryly at the big pot of porridge and other food Jessie had left warming for her. She thought it really wasn't her morning for a big breakfast.

She thought she might make a start on her packing later. She had bought all kinds of souvenirs since she had been in the Highlands and she felt she might need to buy an extra bag to carry them all. One way or another, she thought miserably, she would have plenty of memories of Scotland.

At nine o'clock there was a rapping on the door knocker and she went listlessly into the hall and opened the door. Gordon stood there, in a tweed jacket and polo-necked sweater. He smiled at her.

Fiona stared at him. She had forgotten he had said he would call for her at nine. She hadn't really forgotten, but she had assumed he would know somehow that she discovered him seducing Moyra last night so he wouldn't turn up.

He said, glancing at her dressing gown, 'So you've decided to have a late morning. Was yesterday too much for you?'

She stared at him, her face wrinkling in anguish and disgust. 'You—you—Oh! Go away!' she cried, then slammed the door.

But his foot shot forward and stopped the door closing. 'What the hell——!' he began brusquely as she pushed against the door, trying to close it. Then she was sent reeling as he put his shoulder to the door and forced it open.

'Go away!' she cried as she staggered back into the hall. 'I don't want to see you! You—you—*fornicator*!'

Gordon stepped into the hall, his face dark and his blue eyes smouldering like dry ice. 'I didn't know you knew big words like that,' he snapped.

'But I want to know what you mean—and what's got into you?'

He strode towards her, but she jumped away. He followed her as she retreated into the living room.

'Get out!' she cried. 'I don't want to talk to you!'

He was across the room in three strides and caught her before she could dash into the kitchen.

He seized her by the shoulders and said, taking a deep breath, 'Now calm down, Fiona! You've probably got an explanation for this. I'd like to hear it. Then maybe I can make sense of it.'

She let her head hang and avoided meeting his eyes. She didn't struggle in his grip, because she knew it would be a waste of time. 'I've got nothing to say,' she said shortly, 'Now would you please go. I don't want to see you again—ever!'

He gave her a gentle shake. 'Fiona,' he said quietly. 'I've no intention of leaving until you tell me what's wrong. I thought—after yesterday—that we'd become, say, a little more than friends.'

She threw her head back and glared at him. 'Don't talk about yesterday!' she snapped. 'That's all over! You—you disgust me!'

'O.K.,' he said, his voice controlled. 'Then why do I—digust you?'

'You know perfectly well why!' she flared. 'You know what——' She broke off. 'No, I said I didn't want to talk to you. Go *away*!'

She struggled in his grip and kicked hard at his shins, but as she was only wearing soft fluffy slippers, her kick wasn't very effective. Gordon moved his feet astride, then slid his hands under her armpits and raised her off the ground so her feet kicked uselessly between his legs.

Exasperated, she took the only course left and twisted her head round and down, then bit savagely at his thumb.

He gave a snarl of pain and she regretted her action immediately. An expression of cold fury swept over his hawk-like face.

'Right!' he ground out. 'When we first met I thought you needed a good spanking! And that's what you're going to get if you don't tell me what this is all about!'

'No!' she screamed as he made to hoist her over his shoulder. 'I'll tell you—put me down, you animal!'

He let her slide unceremoniously to her feet where she stood quivering with rage.

'I saw you last night!' she spat. 'I came to your cottage, and I looked in the window and saw you making love to your—model—Moyra!'

His brow cleared slightly, but he still looked puzzled. 'What were you doing outside my cottage?'

'I came to see you!' she spat at him.

'Then why didn't you come in?'

'Oh!' She glared at him. 'You're disgusting! How could I come in, when you were holding her in your arms, kissing her—and she was half naked! What kind of man are you? Did you think I'd sit around and read a book while you made love to her?'

'Moyra wasn't half naked,' he growled. 'She was wearing revealing gear, sure, because she wanted some glamorous, sensual pictures. But I didn't make love to her.'

'That—that passionate embrace I saw—that was just a—a friendly gesture?' She looked at him with loathing and contempt. 'You do that to all your models when you're photographing them?'

'No, I don't. But yes, we did kiss—once. At least, I hate to be ungallant, but it was Moyra who kissed me. For old times' sake,' he added.

'Oh? Then you and she were—lovers?'

He nodded. 'A long time ago. When she was in the States. But that kiss you saw was the only intimate things that's taken place between us since I got here.'

She snorted. 'You must think I'm stupid if you expect me to believe that!'

'Fiona,' he said patiently, 'while I was photographing her, we chatted, as I normally do with my models. I took the opportunity to explain why I hadn't been seeing much of her. I told her about you, and how much you'd—distracted me. We talked about it for a while, then she understood and gave me a friendly kiss while I was changing films.'

'I don't believe you,' she said coldly. 'It certainly didn't look to me like just a—friendly kiss!'

'Look,' he said wearily, 'I've often been kissed by models while I've been working alone with them. I've even kissed them occasionally myself— at the end of an especially good session. You maybe don't understand it, but in glamour photography you must establish a very close rapport between photographer and subject.'

'You were certainly doing that!' Fiona snorted. 'A really *close* rapport!'

He shrugged. 'It's all an act, a big professional act. The models know it—and so does the photographer. But to take sensual pictures you have to get the girl to look at you—meaning the camera—like she was madly in love. That's all there is to it.'

'You're a liar!' she said shortly. 'You didn't try to make me look at the camera like that!'

'No,' he said, 'because I wasn't taking glamour shots of you. They were scenic pictorials.' He grinned suddenly. 'Anyway, I didn't have to ask you to look at the camera as if you were in love. You did it without prompting.'

'Oh!' she cried furiously. 'You're a conceited, egotistical, arrogant, deceitful, revolting, disgusting, foul—male!'

Gordon's grin widened and he reached out his arms to grasp her, but she jumped back, glaring savagely at him.

He said mildly, 'I'd say you're just about ready to fall into my arms.'

Fiona stood choking for a moment, then moved quickly back towards the kitchen door. 'Keep away!' she cried. 'I'm not going to fall into your arms. I don't want you to touch me! I still think you're a liar!'

His brow darkened. 'I don't like that word. I've told you the truth about last night. There's no more to it. I was only doing my job. The pictures are to repay Moyra for her hospitality, that's all.'

'Liar!' she snapped defiantly.

His brow grew black, but he folded his arms and took a deep breath. 'I told you not to call me a liar. I don't like it. In fact I dislike it very much. But I'm sorry I told you I didn't like the word for you're behaving like a little girl name-calling. But don't say it again, or I'll tan your hide! Is that what you want? If you do—then call me a liar once more!'

He stood poised on the balls of his feet, his hands hanging loosely at his sides.

Fiona glared at him, debating, then she licked her lips and opened her mouth, tensing herself, ready to run out the front door.

'Liar!' she mouthed defiantly, then lifted the skirt of her dressing gown and flew like the wind towards the door and down the path straight into Charles' astonished arms.

Charles held her by the shoulders and demanded, 'What on earth——?'

Then he glanced up and saw Gordon striding out of the door.

'Hello, Charles,' Gordon said calmly, 'I was just leaving.'

'Oh?' said Charles, staring at Fiona huddled in his arms, then back to Gordon, who strolled towards them.

'Yes,' Gordon grunted, 'I was just saying goodbye to Fiona.'

As he drew near, Fiona pulled herself closer to Charles, who held her protectively.

Gordon glanced at her briefly, a look of cold contempt on his face.

'Goodbye, Miss Cameron,' he said shortly. 'I always thought Moyra was a pretty good actress. But you leave her for dead.'

He strode past them and down the path.

Charles held Fiona at arm's length and asked, 'What on earth was happening between you?'

'Nothing,' she said, quivering and smoothing her hair. 'Absolutely nothing happened between us.'

CHAPTER NINE

NEXT day was Friday, but Fiona wasn't able to leave Duntochter as she had decided to. One reason was that Charles couldn't get her a sleeper reservation on the train to London. As it was a long overnight trip he had said she must not go until he could get her a sleeping berth. The first he could book was on Saturday's train, so she agreed to wait and go then.

Mrs Stewart was concerned at her decision to leave them earlier than she had planned, but tactfully, she didn't probe too much. All she asked was if her decision to leave prematurely had anything to do with Charles.

Fiona assured her it hadn't. In fact, since he had arrived and saved her from Gordon's thundering wrath yesterday, she was feeling very affectionate towards Charles. He might have occasional drinking lapses, she thought loyally, but at least he was too much of a gentleman ever to threaten to beat a woman—no matter how much she might provoke him. And she had certainly provoked Gordon, she thought bitterly.

Yesterday, after Gordon strode from Elgin House, she had eventually got away from Charles and his concern and puzzlement at what had happened between her and Gordon. She had told Charles she wanted to leave as soon as possible, and later he had told her he couldn't get a sleeper until Saturday.

Fiona had rushed up to her room and thrown herself on her bed and stared bleakly at the ceiling. She had a whole two days to fill before she could get on the train and get back to London and start putting memories of Gordon Ross out of her mind. All day Thursday she wandered around like a ghost, never leaving the house, and both Charles and Mrs Stewart had been concerned about her. Mrs Stewart had wanted to call a doctor, but Fiona had roused herself enough to assure her she didn't need a doctor. She was painfully aware that there never had been and never would be any medical cure for a broken heart.

She had barely slept at all Thursday night, tossing and turning, bitter memories crowding in as she tried to force thoughts of her deceitful lover from her mind. She was glad when dawn finally came on Friday morning and eventually she went down for breakfast with dark half-circles under her eyes, looking pale and gaunt.

Mrs Stewart instantly ascribed her appearance to the fact that she had hardly eaten anything all through the previous day.

She forced Fiona to have a large plate of porridge, virtually standing over her and watching her eat each spoonful. Then she brought in Finnan haddie, steamed as Fiona liked it, and made her eat that too. Fiona begged off any more, except for two cups of tea in the large china cups Jessie used. Like a lot of Scotswomen, Jessie didn't think tea tasted right unless it was served in good china.

It was the day of the planned demonstration against the new highway, and last night Charles had been busy travelling around the district with Hamish and Colin mustering support for the protest and enrolling people to turn up next day.

Last night, Fiona had taken little interest in their plans, she had been too full of her own miseries over her broken love affair.

In the early hours of Friday morning she began reluctantly to wonder if perhaps there was a chance—just the vaguest possibility—that he might be telling the truth and that he and Moyra had only kissed for old times' sake. But she found it hard to believe, remembering how seductive Moyra had looked in her filmy top.

She knew how virile and demanding Gordon could be—the memory of her own near-surrender made her blush. She couldn't imagine him stopping at a kiss. She was prepared to believe that maybe it had been a farewell embrace he and Moyra had been indulging in, but she was sure he wouldn't have been able to resist one last fling with Moyra before she left him and went back to the Castle.

That was if she did go back to the Castle, she thought hotly. Very probably she had stayed the night, sharing his big recessed bed—after they had warmed themselves by the blazing fire.

How could she possibly accept his word that nothing had happened between them? It was expecting too much. Then she thought perhaps she had been foolish running away after she discovered them kissing. She should have waited, hiding herself, and watched to see what they did. But the thought of spying on Gordon made her flush with repugnance. She reflected that it would be hopeless for the woman who married him, knowing he was always going to be around beautiful women, and exposed to temptation, while she sat at home, cooking his dinner and caring for his children and wondering who he was with now.

Yet he had certainly reacted vehemently when she had accused him of lying. But why should it be important for him to convince her he hadn't made love to Moyra? If he didn't care about her— Fiona—why should it matter to him if he lost her?

Perhaps it was just his pride. He didn't like being the one who was shown the door. He much preferred telling the woman it was all over—as he had claimed he had done with Moyra.

Well, Fiona thought grimly, it was all over now. And with luck she wouldn't see him again.

Over breakfast on Friday morning, Charles was talking about the planned demonstration and she decided suddenly she wanted to go. She didn't give her reasons to Charles, but she thought it would be better than moping around the house all day, avoiding Mrs Stewart's anxious ministrations and enquiring looks. Charles said he would be glad to have her there. One more anti-highway person would help swell the crowd for the TV cameras.

'But you've got to keep out of anything active,' he warned her. 'You can carry a placard and wave it at the cameras—but no more. Hamish, Colin and I will be handling the action.'

The official party for the highway dedication was mostly assembled by two o'clock at the Prince's Arms, a tiny hotel beside a big burn on the moors about ten miles from Duntochter.

A large clearing had been gouged out of the lightly-timbered forest through which the highway would be cut. The commemorative stone, covered by a blue silk cloth, stood on one side of the clearing and near it was a trestle table covered by a Union Jack. There was a microphone on a stand on the table with leads running to portable speakers on each side.

A number of wooden benches had been placed in rows in front of the flag-covered table and some people were already sitting on them when Fiona arrived in Mrs Stewart's car with four women from Duntochter she had collected from their homes. Like her, they were anti-highway and talked against it vigorously in broad Scots accents all the way from the village to the Prince's Arms.

Fiona, dressed in blue jeans and a bulky Fair Isle sweater, let her passengers out, then parked the car. The hotel's small parking lot was crammed with vehicles and they spilled out on to the road and were parked haphazardly along the road verge for a hundred yards on each side of the hotel.

The largest and most important cars had brought Sir Angus and some officials from

Inverness. Sir Angus must have dragooned all his guests—and most of his staff—into attending to help form a pro-highway audience. Fiona could see him, standing in the clearing, surrounded by a large group who were obviously on his side. Moyra was there too.

Among the parked vehicles were several trucks which were unloading road workers. From a huge transporter, a big yellow bulldozer was being driven off. Two TV camera vans stood in the parking lot outside the front door of the hotel. With the TV crews were two men carrying large press cameras. Then suddenly she saw Gordon wearing a fleece-lined flying jacket and cord pants, his Nikon hanging from its neckstrap. He was talking with one of the media people and she moved quickly away before he could spot her.

She walked across the road to the clearing, watching for Charles, Hamish and Colin. At the rear of the clearing, parked among the pine trees, she saw two black police cars. Sergeant MacGregor was standing near the official table. Behind her, Fiona heard a cool voice say, 'And where are your radical friends today?'

She turned and saw Moyra, who surveyed her with cold disdain. She was wearing a straight black suede skirt and a square matching suede jacket wrapped at the front. She looked poised and very beautiful. She studied Fiona in her well-worn jeans and sweater, then added disdainfully, 'You look every inch an agitator. Still planning to interfere in other people's business?'

'Saving the Highlands from being spoiled is

everyone's business!' Fiona snapped.

'You come from twelve thousand miles away,' Moyra said tartly. 'It's hardly your concern.'

'My forefathers lived in this area generations before yours did!' Fiona said hotly. 'It is my concern!'

'Everything's your concern,' Moyra said, tight-lipped. 'Even my guests!'

'What do you mean?'

'You know exactly what I mean—Gordon Ross. You've thrown yourself at him ever since you saw him!' Her face twisted into a scowl and suddenly she didn't look so beautiful. She spat out, 'I'm warning you—leave him alone! I've known him a long time—much longer than you have—and I won't stand by and see him snatched away by—by—a child like you!'

Fiona stared. 'I thought you didn't care about him any more?'

Moyra's eyes narrowed. 'Is that what he told you? If he did, he's wrong. I care about him very much. Too much to let him throw himself away on a—colonial dolly-bird!'

Fiona ignored the colonial taunt. New Zealand wasn't a colony any more. Instead she said, with cold dignity, 'I think your information is out of date. I have no interest in Gordon Ross. He's a brute and a liar and I hate the sight of him. So——' she forced a grimace—'he's all yours. And you're welcome to him!'

'Thank you,' Moyra said frostily, 'but I don't need anyone to—to pass a man on to me. I'm quite capable of taking him away from anyone who thinks she's won him.'

'Yes,' Fiona said shortly, 'you did that very well.'

She turned on her heel and strode back on to the road towards the cars of the anti-highway people.

As she did so, there was a tooting of horns and a small procession of three vehicles came along the road from Duntochter. First was a Land Rover driven by Charles. Second was an estate car driven by Hamish and behind was a flat-bodied truck driven by Colin and packed with what looked like farm workers and their women-folk. The Land Rover and estate car both had flags flying from their roofs. One was a large yellow Scottish standard with its red lion rampant and the other was the blue and white St Andrew's cross of Scotland.

A number of people got out of the Land Rover as it pulled up and they began to unload placards. On both sides of the vehicle were large signs which read, in foot-high red letters, 'DON'T DESTROY THE HIGHLANDS!' and 'STOP NEEDLESS ROAD BUILDING'.

Charles got out and Fiona ran up to him and he smiled. He looked excited. He said gleefully, 'We've got a much bigger crowd than I expected. We'll be able to put on a really good show for the TV cameras. We'll give Sir Angus and his cronies a bit of a fright!'

The anti-highway people were milling around the cars trying to get a placard or to take a corner of several long calico banners that were unrolled.

Fiona slipped into Charles' seat and managed to grab a small placard before they were all seized by eager hands. It was one she had lettered herself at Hamish's place and read, not very originally, 'STOP—NO ROAD!'

Over in the clearing where Sir Angus and the official party stood; Fiona could see them looking contemptuously at the milling demonstrators. In front of the hotel, the TV camera crews started their vans and drove them across the road towards the clearing.

When the Land Rover was unloaded, Charles drove it forward and bumped off the road on to the clearing, then reversed the vehicle so its nose was pointing back towards the road. He parked it fairly close to the official table and the veiled stone.

The protesters began assembling in the clearing near the Land Rover which was to be their rallying point. The TV vans had been positioned behind the benches, while the bulldozer had been driven to the far side of the clearing. The TV cameramen on top of the vans swung their cameras in an arc, checking that they could cover everything from their high vantage points.

Sir Angus and his party still stood on the other side of the clearing, although most of the people who had been with him had taken seats on the benches. Apparently one VIP from Inverness was still to arrive.

Fiona was overcome by a sudden desire to go to the toilet and she squeezed through the throng and hurried across the road to the hotel. When she came out, still carrying her placard, she almost bumped into Gordon, who looked at her frowning. 'I see you're going to be in the thick of it again.'

She tried to push past him, but he barred her. She snapped, 'Are you going to try and beat me? There are police here, so you won't be able to!'

He looked at her darkly, 'Just don't get involved today!'

She choked with rage. 'Thank you, but I don't take orders from you!'

He shrugged. 'Then take some advice. Don't hit anybody with your placard—especially not a cop.'

Fiona glared at him and stalked off across the gravel parking area towards the road, her red hair in its ponytail bobbing against the back of her bulky sweater, her bottom in the tight jeans quivering with rage. She looked as if she was spoiling for a fight.

The official from Inverness had arrived and joined Sir Angus behind the flag-draped table. The master of ceremonies adjusted the microphone, then began to talk at length about what an auspicious occasion it was for the people of Duntochter and district.

Finally he got round to introducing Sir Angus, who got to his feet and seized the microphone. Black beard jutting aggressively, he began by giving details of the highway project. He was a much better speaker than the M.C. and his booming voice, amplified over the portable speakers, commanded attention.

He made several scathing references to short-sighted people who opposed the highway, glancing pointedly at the placard-waving group surrounding the Land Rover.

Amid booing and counter-clapping from those in favour of the highway, Sir Angus finally got round to the reason he was there.

He said, 'It gives me great pleasure to unveil this commemorative stone. After that, Mr MacKinnon of the Roads and Works Department will drive the bulldozer and cut the first sods which will be the route of the highway.'

He strode forward and took the unveiling cord in his hand. On the roof of the TV vans, the cameramen focussed on the stone as Sir Angus bellowed, 'I now declare this highway construction project officially launched.'

He tugged at the cord and the veil fell to the ground, revealing the obelisk with its inscribed brass plate.

There was a ripple of applause, then a barrage of boos and catcalls from the demonstrators.

On the other side of the clearing, the bulldozer's diesel engine roared into life and Sir Angus and the official party strode towards the big machine which was surrounded by road workers and engineers.

The TV cameras swung towards the bulldozer as Mr MacKinnon from Inverness climbed on board.

Fiona saw Hamish take a portable battery megaphone from the back of the Land Rover, and followed by a group of placard-waving demonstrators, he pushed his way through the crowd until he reached the bulldozer. With his supporters behind him, he strode to the front of the bulldozer and his group, a mixed bunch of men and women, promptly sat down on the turf in front of the shining blade of the huge machine.

Then she heard Hamish's amplified voice above the roar of the bulldozer's engine.

'This is a shameful day for the Highlands! This project will spell the ruin of our way of life and the devastation of our land.'

He went on in the same vein and there was a lot of cheering from those around him and from the other protestors who had remained near the Land Rover where Fiona was.

She could see Sergeant MacGregor moving ponderously through the crowd towards Hamish and the seated protestors. In the background, the other police had got out of their cars and were standing by.

The bulldozer was now the centre of attention, but more than a dozen people, including Colin and Charles, stayed near the Land Rover. Then Charles nodded to Colin and climbed in behind the wheel and started the Land Rover's engine. Colin, with two young men helping him, swiftly attached a wire rope to the tow bar at the rear of the Land Rover and ran the rope towards the stone. They hitched the rope around the stone and slid its loop tight with a metal clip. Then Colin waved to Charles, who had his head out of the cabin, looking back.

He revved the motor and peat flew from under

the vehicle's rear wheels as it moved forward, taking up the slack in the rope. Charles revved harder and the stone toppled from its base and slowly the Land Rover dragged it across the turf.

The vehicle reached the road and started across it, the stone bumping behind on the rope. Charles could have crossed the road and driven down to the burn without being spotted, but that wasn't the intention. They wanted the TV cameras to cover what they were doing with the stone.

Colin cupped his hands to his mouth and bellowed towards the throng around the bulldozer, 'Hey, the stone's been taken!'

It was a few seconds before what he said penetrated the noise, then his cry was taken up— 'They've taken the stone!'

The protesters sitting in front of the bulldozer sprang to their feet and swarmed across the clearing to follow the Land Rover.. The TV crews quickly started their vans and bumped over the turf to follow the stone.

Sir Angus and his party also began to run after the stone, and Fiona saw Sergeant MacGregor put his whistle to his mouth and blow three sharp blasts. The waiting policemen left their cars and strode purposefully across the clearing.

Fiona joined Colin and a group of placard-waving demonstrators and they rushed after the stone, which by this time had been towed close to the edge of the burn.

Then the police, Sir Angus and his group and Hamish and his supporters all reached the Land

Rover at the same time and a near-brawl developed around the stone.

Fiona found herself close to Hamish, who was using his megaphone to urge on the protesters. Fiona could see Sir Angus struggling with a man holding a placard and she also caught a brief glimpse of Moyra. She was taking no part in the fracas, but was standing near the hotel, a look of contempt on her face as she watched the disturbance.

Hamish's voice over the megaphone was deafening and a beefy, perspiring policeman lumbered up and growled, 'Cut out that noise!'

Hamish ignored him and bellowed through the mouthpiece for more protesters to help dump the stone in the burn.

The policeman closed with Hamish and tried to wrench the megaphone from his hands. Hamish resisted vigorously and punches flew. 'Right!' the constable panted, 'I'm taking you in!'

Fiona struck out at the policeman with her placard. 'Leave him alone!' she cried. 'He's not breaking the law!'

As he struggled with Hamish, the policeman grunted, 'Keep out of this, miss, or you might get hurt. And don't strike me again or I'll arrest you too!'

He managed to get an arm lock on Hamish and twisted his arm behind his back. Hamish grunted with pain and Fiona flew at the policeman, kicking at his shins and hitting him with the placard.

As the policeman relaxed his grip on Hamish to defend himself against the furious girl, Hamish twisted free and bellowed through the megaphone, almost in the policeman's face, 'Rally round me, men! Let's sink the stone!'

Exasperated, the beefy constable knocked the megaphone from Hamish's grasp and Hamish made a dive for it at the same time as the policeman did. Fiona dived after them, clinging to the policeman's legs as they all sprawled on the muddy turf.

Then suddenly she felt herself lifted by two strong arms, and, kicking and struggling, she was spun round and saw it was Gordon who was holding her.

'Let me go!' she squealed. 'Put me down!'

'You're getting out of this!' he snapped, 'or you'll end up in jail.'

He slid his hands down her waist, lifted her and tossed her over one shoulder.

She thrashed her legs and beat helplessly on his back with her hands as he strode quickly away from the mêlée and up past the hotel. One arm held her pinned to his shoulder while the other gripped her flailing legs.

As she twisted in his grip, throwing her head from side to side and yelling at him, she was vaguely aware of Moyra's face as they passed the hotel. Her brow was black as she glared at the struggling Fiona, hanging over Gordon's shoulder.

He strode rapidly along the road, then stopped and put her down beside his Land Rover. He held her by her ponytail so she couldn't escape.

'I'm getting tired of manhandling you,' he grunted as he tugged the door of the vehicle open.

'Now quit struggling and get in, or I'll stuff you in like a sack of potatoes!'

She opened her mouth to protest, but he picked her up and bundled her in past the wheel, then slid in beside her and started the motor.

'Don't try and get out!' he snapped. 'I'd catch you before you got the door open.'

He put the vehicle in gear and drove it off the road verge, then accelerated. He looked at her as she stared back sullenly. 'You'll thank me for this later,' he growled. 'Keeping you out of prison.'

He glanced at her as he slipped into top gear and the Land Rover sped away from the mêlée.

Fiona glared at him and snapped, 'Nothing you could do for me would make me thank you!'

His eyes glinted dangerously. 'We'll see about that, Miss Cameron. Very soon.'

CHAPTER TEN

GORDON didn't take Fiona to Elgin House as she demanded that he do. He drove through Duntochter village in that direction, but when they reached the gates of the Castle he swung the Land Rover into the drive past old Wullie, who nodded affably and touched his bonnet.

Fiona cried, 'I want to go home! I don't want to come here!'

'You'll stay at my cottage for a while,' he said brusquely, 'until everything blows over. If I took you to the Stewarts' you'd get back to the protest some way—or go to the police station and start your own protest.'

'That's exactly what I want to do!' she exclaimed. 'Get out and help my friends. You've no right to bring me here!'

He glanced at her indignant, seething face as they sped along the gravel drive, then turned off on to the track leading to his cottage.

'Sadly,' he drawled, 'might is often right. And I'm mightier than you.'

'You mean stronger!' she spat contemptuously. 'I weigh eight stone and you weigh about thirteen—and you're taller than me. No wonder you can pick me up whenever you like and throw me around. It must make you feel very masculine—and cowardly!'

Gordon nodded. 'O.K., I weigh one hundred and eighty pounds and you weigh a hundred and ten. So what? You fight like a hellcat! But because you're a girl, I have to pull my punches and be gentle.'

'Gentle!' she choked as the Land Rover stopped with a squeal of brakes outside his cottage. 'You call how you treat me gentle? You're a—a brute!'

He smiled coldly and slid out his door, then leaned across the seats and pulled her out with him. Soft, misty rain had began to fall and the afternoon had turned grey and dull.

He gripped her arm and drew her towards the cottage door. 'Come on, I'll make some coffee.'

'I don't *want* coffee!' she snapped as she was forced across the gravel to the cottage where he opened the door then thrust her inside. 'I want to go home!'

He closed the door, turned the key, then removed it and slid it into a pocket in his flying jacket.

'Shut up and sit down,' he said coldly. 'You're not going anywhere for a while.'

'This is—is kidnapping!' Fiona snapped.

He smiled. 'No, abduction. In the old Highland days I'd have thrown you over my saddle and galloped off. Then, back in my lair, I'd have had my way with you.'

He unzipped his flying jacket and tossed it over a chair. Then he held out his arms and moved towards her.

She leapt back. 'Don't you touch me!'

Gordon paused. 'Why? What would you do if I did?'

'I—I'd scream—and fight. I'd——'

'Screaming won't do any good, tucked away here. It's a mile to the Castle and a mile to the gate—and old Wullie's part deaf. So maybe you'll settle for a cup of coffee?'

'All right,' she said sullenly, 'I'll have one cup.'

He nodded. 'O.K., come into the scullery while I make it.'

He waited until Fiona moved mutinously into the tiny scullery and she stood glowering by the door of the darkroom while he made coffee.

She reflected savagely that this was the third time she had been in his cottage. And two out of three times she had been brought against her will. The one occasion she had come voluntarily— after the dance—she had sat on his knee by the firelight and he had kissed her for the first time. Well, she thought grimly, there would be no kissing this time. In fact, she wouldn't even talk to him any more. She knew that whatever he might do, there was no way he could force her to talk. She grimaced. She felt like the heroine of a gangster movie—he wouldn't make her talk.

She thought bitterly that trying to beat him verbally only played into his hands. He was quick with his responses and invariably made her feel at a disadvantage. Also, he controlled himself better than she did, so she always seemed to end by childishly poking her tongue at him. Well, he wouldn't get that satisfaction any more. She'd remain absolutely mute.

Gordon poured the coffee, then motioned her to follow him back into the living room. He carried the two mugs over to the fireside and nodded for her to take one of the easy chairs. Fiona sat down and he handed her a mug, putting his own down by the fireplace. He picked up the poker and stirred the fire until it crackled and blazed.

Outside, a flurry of rain splattered against the windows and he remarked, 'Getting almost like winter now.'

She said nothing, but took a sip of her coffee.

He looked at her. 'Like some wine? Old Wullie's home brew?'

She looked disdainfully away.

'I see,' he drawled, 'so you plan to be silent. Well, that's a change. But your throat probably needs a rest, after the way you were screaming at the protest.'

She bit off a retort and swallowed hard.

He stood up. 'If you won't talk, then I'll show you some pictures. They might interest you.'

He went out into the scullery and she heard the darkroom door being opened.

She glanced quickly at the tiny windows and wondered if she could get across the room, open a window and squeeze out before he came back. But she doubted if she'd make it—and it would only give Gordon an excuse to manhandle her again and drag her back.

He came out of the scullery with a batch of prints in one hand. He sat down and spread the pictures on the rug, fanning them in a semi-circle around her feet.

'These are some of the shots I took of Moyra the other night,' he said carelessly. 'I thought they might interest you.'

Fiona glanced down coldly at the pictures. In spite of her feelings about him—and Moyra—she had to admit that the photos were very good. Even working under difficulties as he had done, with only two floodlights and no studio equipment, the pictures made Moyra look very glamorous. They were mostly head and shoulder shots and were sensual but tasteful. Moyra must have changed her clothes several times, for the photos showed her in a variety of seductive sweaters, low-cut blouses and even a revealing negligee.

'Moyra is very pleased with them,' Gordon told her. 'I'll give her the negatives so she can get prints run off for publicity purposes. What do you think of them?'

Fiona stared down at the pictures, but said nothing.

'Personally,' he said easily, 'I like the ones I took of you better. You're an amateur, but you've got that unspoiled freshness people like. You could pose for most kinds of shot—but Moyra is strictly the high fashion, glamour-puss type.'

Pointedly, she turned her head away and looked into the blazing fire.

Gordon dropped to his knees, scooped up the pictures from around her feet and placed them in a pile to one side. He moved closer and sat by her knees, and she promptly jerked her legs away. He placed one hand on her knee and she hunched back into her chair and stared at him, her expression one of loathing.

He moved closer until he was leaning comfortably against her chair. He squeezed her knee and she jumped.

'Now—about us,' he said.

Fiona pushed his hand from her knee and tossed her head then stared at the fire.

He took one of her hands and she tried to snatch it away, but he held it firmly.

'You're behaving childishly again,' he growled. 'You're not leaving until everything is O.K. between us. Even if I have to keep you here all night.'

She stifled an exclamation and he looked at her speculatively.

'That's not a bad idea,' he drawled. 'It's pretty cold these nights. And I get chilly in that big bed, all alone.'

She glared at him, almost exploding with the effort of not retorting.

Gordon taunted her, 'Simon says you can talk.'

Fiona just scowled at him and stared into the fire.

He grunted and released her hand which she snatched away. She folded both hands across her bosom. Suddenly he placed a large hand round both her ankles and tugged sharply so that she slithered from the chair on to the rug beside him. Then arms like a bear's went round her and she was cradled helplessly in his embrace, writhing furiously but ineffectively. One hand caught her by the ponytail and pulled her head back, then he bent his head and kissed her tightly-closed lips while she seethed against him.

She found it difficult to breathe as she let herself lie stiffly in his arms, keeping her mouth tightly closed. But his lips played with hers, teasing them, until finally she gasped explosively and opened her mouth to suck in air.

Then his firm mouth crushed her soft open lips and she arched her body as his hand stroked her neck, playing with her ear lobes, then sliding down the back of her neck under her sweater to tickle her shoulders.

She gave a smothered sigh, then her body went limp and relaxed. Like a gamefish that had fought to the finish, she had had enough. There was no resistance left in her.

Gordon pulled her down on to the rug and cradled her head in his arms as he stretched himself alongside her. He muttered into her ear, 'You're an absolute menace, Fiona. You're wild, crazy and impulsive. You annoy the hell out of me more than any female I've ever met. Yet I can't seem to get you out of my life—which is what I should do if I had any brains!'

Fiona allowed herself to sneak a glance at his face. His eyes were deep dark grey, and very tender.

He shook his head as he gazed at her. 'I don't know what to do about you,' he muttered. 'I've abducted you—twice now—proved that you're no match for me, yet you still won't do as I say.'

The words came out of her like an explosion. 'Why should I do what you say?'

Gordon smiled as she broke her self-imposed

silence. Then he murmured, 'Because I'm bigger than you, older than you, wiser than you—and I'm a man.'

'Chauvinist pig!' she spat.

He looked at her sorrowfully. 'I guess there's only one thing left to do with you.' He sat up suddenly and leaned over and seized one of her ankles, sliding her brogue off.

'What are you doing?' she cried, struggling.

'Taking off your shoes,' he said coolly. 'They're wet and muddy.'

Fiona tried to kick, but he held her firmly and slid off her other shoe. Then he got lithely to his feet and kicked off his own shoes.

She stared up at him as she lay sprawled on the rug. 'What are you going to do?' she cried, her eyes wide.

He bent and scooped her up in his arms as if she was a chaff bag and carried her towards the big bed in the wall.

She redoubled her struggles as he strode to the bed. But it was a waste of time. He tossed her on the bed and threw himself beside her on top of the big eiderdown.

'Move over!' he commanded as she scrambled across his body, trying to get out of the bed.

As she struggled on top of him he wound his arms around her and pulled her against him so she was stretched full length along his hard body.

'Keep struggling,' he drawled. 'It's making me very excited.'

'Oh!' Fiona stopped writhing and tried to slide from his body, but he held her pinned on top of himself and she averted her face which was only inches above his mocking lips.

He slid one hand behind her neck and forced her lips down to meet his. Suddenly, for the second time, all resistance left her and she sighed and collapsed against him. It was an absolute waste of time trying to fight the brute.

This time Gordon kissed her very tenderly and his arms were gentle as he stroked her back. She gave a long, shuddering sigh as he turned her on to her side and cradled her head in one arm as he ranged himself alongside her, still kissing her gently yet ardently.

Then he took his lips away and murmured, 'Comfortable?' She gave a small nod. He smiled. 'It beats the hell out of running around a soggy moor, or lying in a blanket in the rain.'

She mumbled something and he said, 'This is a perfect way to spend a rainy afternoon.'

She muttered, 'I don't know why you want to spend it with me. You've been so nasty to me. You treat me badly—and you're rough and horrible.'

He stroked her hair, one hand undoing her ponytail and letting her tresses hang free. 'You're quite a handful for any man. I've never known a girl like you.'

She settled in his arms. 'Do you always threaten to beat your girl-friends? Or am I the only one?'

He shook his head. 'No, you're the first. I guess you must bring out the beast in me.' He kissed her lightly on the forehead.

'Why do I do that?' she asked earnestly.

'Because you're so stubborn and pigheaded. How did your father control you when you were growing up?'

She murmured, 'I was always a very good girl for my father.'

'But he must have had to—chastise you, sometimes?'

'Well, yes, once or twice. He did spank me occasionally.'

'You must have deserved it.'

'I don't know if I did. I can't remember.'

'I guess you must have got him pretty mad,' mused Gordon, 'same as you got me.'

'Well, I was furious with you. Because I thought you were a liar!' Her hand flew to her lips and she cried, 'Oh, I'm sorry, I mustn't call you that!'

He nodded. 'No, you mustn't. But in fun it's O.K. And this is fun, isn't it?'

He kissed her again and she found herself melting into his arms. She thought resignedly that she must be crazy. She didn't know why she was forgiving him or why she was lying here on his bed responding to his lovemaking. Then she told herself she did know why. One, because she had no choice and two, because she loved and wanted him.

As she returned his kisses with growing passion he caressed her bosom through the thick wool of her sweater.

'What have you got under this?' he murmured, bunching the wool in his hand.

'Only me,' she whispered.

He slid one hand down, then slipped it under her sweater and stroked her tummy, tickling her navel with one finger.

Her skin tingled and his hand slid higher until it gently cupped one of her breasts. He kissed her with a sudden fiery urgency that almost overwhelmed her.

For a long time they embraced while their passion rapidly mounted. Fiona became flushed and hot. Gordon gently slid her sweater up over her shoulders and head and she offered no resistance. Gently he tossed the garment aside, then stroked her breasts and kissed them.

He shucked off his shirt, then drew her soft bosom against his chest and she writhed against him, panting.

She gave a shuddering sigh and murmured, 'Please stop—for a little while.'

'Why?' he asked, nuzzling her ear.

'Because I—I want to enjoy this moment.'

'You'll enjoy it even more if I keep going,' he murmured.

'I know. But I—it's lovely. I feel so—so snug and secure. Perhaps I'll never feel so secure again for the rest of my life.'

He kissed her and she sighed, 'Just listen to the rain.'

Outside, the rain pattered against the window panes. Gordon hadn't turned on the lamp and only a pale grey lambency came from the windows while the flickering firelight made dancing patterns of pink and yellow on the walls and ceiling.

'This is what the Scots call the gloaming,' she

said softly. 'Isn't it a nice word? Between daylight and dark, but not yet dusk. It's a beautiful time.'

He held her close, her bare bosom crushed against his chest, while one hand traced the curve of her spine.

He murmured, 'It is a beautiful time.'

He kissed her tenderly, then turned her so she was lying on her back. He raised himself on to one elbow and stroked her hair with his other hand.

'Your eyes have gone greeny-black,' he murmured. 'Like caviare. Not the Scandinavian stuff, but the Beluga.'

Fiona smiled as she stroked his cheek. 'I don't know the difference. I've never had caviare.'

He raised one eyebrow. 'Hmm, then I'll have to remedy that. Maybe tomorrow. You look like you could develop a taste for occasional luxuries.'

'I'm sure I could,' she said, 'if I had someone to teach me.'

'Hmm. On the other hand, maybe I'd better leave you as you are—natural and unspoiled. I don't see you as the caviare type, with a Sobranie in one hand and a glass of Stolichnaya in the other.'

She sighed. 'You're very superior. What's a Sobranie and what's Stolichnaya?'

'A Balkan cigarette and Russian vodka.'

'Hmm. Well, that's three things I've never had—caviare, a cigarette and vodka. I suppose the girls you go around with use these things all the time?'

Gordon nodded. 'They think it displays

sophistication. Like Paris gowns, Porsches and French perfurme.'

She sighed again. 'Three more things I've never had. I'm beginning to feel like a—a little provincial hick.'

He grinned suddenly and kissed her tenderly. 'I hope you never try to become sophisticated. I like you as you are. At this moment, you are just perfect.'

She glanced down at her crumpled jeans—all she was wearing—and muttered, 'You're easily pleased.'

He smiled. 'You look—what's the Scots word? Fey, I think.'

She said softly, 'I know what that means.'

'Go on—what does it mean?'

'I think it means having second sight or something. Or looking as if you have second sight.'

'Yes. I think they mean a person who can see things that most people can't. Because they're a little out of this world.' His hand played idly with the zipper of her jeans.

'Oh! And you think I'm like that?' She placed one hand over his, preventing him sliding the zipper.

Gordon smiled. 'In some ways. You're a very bewitching mixture of guileless honesty and pig-headed determination. Like you were today at the highway protest.'

Her hand flew to her mouth and she exclaimed, 'Oh, lord! I've forgotten all about Charles and the others! I must find out what happened to them. They'll think I'm terrible!'

She sat up suddenly and struggled free of his enveloping arms. Then, nimbly, in her tight jeans, she slithered over his body and leaped from the bed.

She found her sweater and pulled it over her head, then skipped to the fireside and got her shoes and began to slip them on.

Gordon raised his eyes and grunted, then got off the bed and followed her, pulling on his shirt resignedly.

'You don't have to go back to Elgin House,' he said cajolingly. 'Stay and have supper with me. Why don't I run you down to old Wullie's place? There's a phone there and you can call Elgin House and find how things went. Then, if everything's O.K., we can come back here and have supper.'

She hesitated and he walked over and knelt beside her as she finished putting on her shoes.

He took her face in his hands and kissed her tenderly, murmuring, 'Our conversation was just getting interesting. I planned to tell you some other things.'

'Oh! Well, I suppose I——'

He stroked her cheek. 'Please?' he said softly.

Fiona took a deep breath. His plea left her weak. It was the first time he had actually said please to her about anything. And he was on his knees before her, his eyes actually pleading. She couldn't resist him.

'All right,' she said, melting against his shoulder. 'We'll do that.'

He kissed her lingeringly and she needed all her willpower to push him away and stand up. He put on his shoes and flying jacket, then unlocked the door.

He smiled as he turned the key. 'I don't need to keep you locked in any more.'

Fiona snuggled under his arm as they went outside.

Old Wullie welcomed them and Fiona used the phone and called Elgin House. Charles wasn't there, but Mrs Stewart was, and she gave Fiona all the news.

Apparently the protesters had succeeded in dropping the stone into a deep pool, and after that things had fizzled out. The light rain that had begun falling had helped dampen emotions on the exposed moor. The police had contented themselves with arresting Hamish and he had been taken to Duntochter where Charles had bailed him out. Mrs Stewart said, disapprovingly, that she gathered her son and his friends were now in the village celebrating their victory.

Jessie asked if Fiona was all right and she said she was—and that she was staying with a friend for supper after which she would be home.

Fiona relayed all this to Gordon, who nodded and said he thought the police had been pretty tolerant. 'Different from some countries I've been in, where they'd have used batons and guns and arrested dozens.'

As they stood in the dark outside Wullie's cottage, there was the sudden report of a gun far off in the woods inside the estate.

'Poachers,' said Wullie. 'They've started early.'

Gordon said, 'You mean the poachers come in and shoot Sir Angus's game?'

Wullie growled, 'Naw. One of the poachers might have tripped a gun trap. McKechnie and his men sometimes set trip wires that fire a gun into the air and lets them know the poachers are on the job. Then they chase them.'

Gordon nodded. 'Quite a running battle you have here.'

Wullie grunted. 'A lot of village folk still think they're entitled to take game wherever they can find it. And putting up walls and fences disnae stop them.'

Gordon helped Fiona into the Land Rover, thanked Wullie for the use of the phone and got in behind the wheel.

He drove with one hand and held her with the other until they reached the cottage. When they got out and walked to the cottage door he stopped and took her into his arms. He kissed her, then said softly, 'I'm going to carry you across the threshold.'

She murmured, 'That would be nice. I'll always remember this cottage.'

'It's a perfect honeymoon cottage,' he said. Then he added quietly, 'Will you stay with me tonight?'

Fiona hesitated, then shook her head. 'No,' she whispered. 'I must go back after we have supper. Charles will want to talk about today. And I'm still his guest. I have to go back.'

He nodded, then lifted her easily into his arms,

pressed the latch and kicked the door open. He carried her into the cottage, lit only by the firelight, then set her down gently near the hearth and kissed her tenderly.

She felt her defences crumbling, but managed to push him away a little and murmur, 'You said supper—remember?'

Reluctantly he released her, and shucked off his bulky flying jacket and tossed it over one of the armchairs. 'O.K., supper it is. I'll see what I've got.'

She skipped away from him and scooped up his jacket and smoothed it as he moved towards the scullery.

Gordon paused at the scullery door and said, 'I think I've only got crackers and soup. How does that appeal?'

'Fine, I'd like that. I'd like to see how you cook.'

He grinned. 'If you call heating a can cooking!' Ducking his head, he went into the scullery.

Carrying his jacket, Fiona walked over to the bedside and switched on the lamp, then opened the wardrobe doors to hang his jacket.

She moved his clothes aside to find a hanger and her eyes were drawn instantly to a small red and green-striped Gucci suitcase on top of the low drawers in the wardrobe. It was obviously a woman's case and on it lay a frothy, peach-coloured nightdress.

She let his jacket drop to the floor, and, stunned, she picked up the nightdress between two fingers and stared at it disbelievingly.

Behind her, she heard his voice, 'You can have tomato soup or chicken noodle. And I've got a bottle of wine——'

He stopped talking as she swung to face him, her face white, her eyes staring as she flicked the nightdress off the case and it frothed out as she held it at arm's length.

She said, choking, 'And I suppose this is Moyra's?'

Gordon strode towards her and held out his arms. He had a can of soup in each hand.

'Yes,' he said sharply, 'I suppose it is.'

'I didn't think it was yours!' she flared, throwing the flimsy garment to the floor.

He tossed the soup cans on to an easy chair and strode towards her. 'Fiona,' he said evenly, 'don't blow your top!'

But she jumped towards the bed, then whirled away from it in the direction of the door. She cried out as she backed away, 'I'd like to hear you explain why she keeps her things in your wardrobe!'

He raised his eyes and said slowly, 'I'm not sure I can. She brought some clothes for our photo session the other night, but as far as I recall she took them away with her when she left.'

Fiona stared at him as he glanced at the Gucci case in the wardrobe and the nightdress lying on the floor.

'Huh!' she cried, 'you expect me to believe you haven't looked in your wardrobe since then!'

His frown deepened. 'I don't understand it. Her stuff wasn't there when I left here this afternoon to go to the protest.'

She snorted disbelievingly. 'You're trying to say she put them here while you were out?'

He nodded. 'Maybe while we've been out. I don't know. It's got me beat.'

She moved towards the door. 'You're disgusting!' she cried. 'I hate you!'

Gordon said brusquely, 'Now don't be stupid! Don't say any more. Let's sit down calmly and talk about this.'

She stared at him, her breasts heaving. 'I don't want to talk about it. I've been a fool—a terrible fool!'

'Fiona!' he exclaimed, striding towards her.

She hurried back to the door.

'Keep away from me!' she cried. 'Don't try to touch me! You've lied to me from the beginning! I hate and despise you!'

His hands dropped to his side and he made no attempt to detain her. 'You're being very stupid!' he said harshly. 'It can easily be explained. I think——'

'Explained!' she cried. 'Yes, I'm sure you can explain anything. It's very easy when you're a—a liar!'

She spat out the word, then turned and ran choking into the night.

CHAPTER ELEVEN

FIONA rushed blindly from the cottage and dashed down the track and along the drive in the direction of the gates. After a few yards, she swerved suddenly and plunged into the thick woods that bordered the drive. She thought she should keep off the drive, as very likely Gordon would chase her in the Land Rover, and, remembering his threat last time she had called him a liar, she didn't relish the prospect of him catching her. He might really beat her this time, but even if he didn't, she couldn't face the humiliation of being caught and bundled into the Land Rover, then taken back to the cottage while he forced her to listen to his 'explanation'.

She laughed, a choking, sobbing laugh, as she ran through the bushes, away from the drive, then turned and ran through the undergrowth in the general direction of the gates.

Explanation! That was funny. What did he have to explain? Plenty, she thought, but how could he explain Moyra's nightdress and her other things? She almost threw up as she ran, panting through the trees. All the time he had been wooing her, Moyra's things had been stashed in his wardrobe waiting for her next visit. It was revolting, she thought, choking with rage.

Oh, he had been very clever. He had admitted

he had had an affair with Moyra—in America. But it had all been over for a long time, he had told her, and like a fool she had believed him. How stupid girls were when they fell in love, she thought, gasping as she crashed through a thicket. They would believe any lie a man told them. Well, she was lucky, she'd found out about him in time.

He must think she was a fool, she thought, panting, trying to act as if he didn't know Moyra's things had been there all along. And trying to say that Moyra must have sneaked into his cottage and put her things there while they were out. Why would Moyra do that? She had nothing to fear from Fiona. For what did she have that Moyra didn't have? Only one thing—what Gordon had said himself: she was fresh and unspoiled. In his kind of life, mixing with glamorous women all the time, he probably never met girls like her. So he had set out to amuse himself during his Highland idyll and use her for his pleasure. But he wasn't going to break completely with Moyra. Oh, no— he wanted them both!

Fiona shuddered as she recalled how she had nearly given herself to him, yesterday in the heather and this afternoon when she had lain on his bed. But each time she had managed to resist his experienced lovemaking.

She berated herself as she ran, twisting and turning to avoid obstacles in the dark. What a stupid fool she'd been! She had even let herself dream of marrying him—as if he would ever have asked her.

Why on earth would he want to marry a pro-

vincial girl like her when he had his pick of some
of the world's most glamorous women? What
would they have talked about once he had sated
himself with her? Beluga caviare? Porsche cars?
Russian vodka? She knew it was only since
coming to London that she had developed even a
modicum of sophistication or worldliness. She
had only ever stayed at a big hotel one night in
her life, and that was when she arrived in London
before she found a flat. But Gordon routinely
lived in such places—or in places like the Castle.
She thought wryly, he was so ultra-sophisticated
he even passed up an invitation to stay at the
Castle and instead opted for a cottage in the
grounds.

But she had already worked out why he preferred the cottage. For he could have Moyra there
quite freely—and any other woman he wanted to
take there. Like herself.

Oh, she thought, her breath coming in great
panting sobs, I was *lucky*!

She plunged on through light, misty rain, her
pace becoming slower as she became winded and
tried to avoid the prickly bramble bushes. Her
chest was heaving and she panted heavily. Soon
she would stop her mad flight and get back on to
the drive, then sneak past old Wullie and out on
to the road.

Just what she would do then she wasn't sure.
Walk, she supposed. It wouldn't be wise to try
and hitch a ride. Not at night on a lonely country
road—even in peaceful Scotland.

She slowed her pace to a walk and strode back

towards the drive. As she did so, she heard the sound of a car motor. It sounded like the Land Rover, but she wasn't going to wait to find out. Instead, she turned and hurried back into the woods.

She planned to walk in a wide arc that would take her into the woods and out again near Wullie's cottage, and she lengthened her stride as she forced her way through the bushes.

Suddenly she tripped over something in the dark and there was an explosive roar above her head as a shotgun discharged. She gave a scream of fright, then stumbled over a root and sprawled full-length in the mud.

Then everything seemed to happen at once. A flashlight beam shone out of the dark and lit up her sprawling figure and a voice with a broad Scottish accent called out, 'Don't move, you brazen thief, or I'll fill you with buckshot!'

Terrified, she glanced up and behind the flashlight she dimly made out the figures of two men in canvas gaiters and leather jackets. They were carrying shotguns. They crashed through the undergrowth towards her, then halted. Fiona scrambled to her feet, winded but unhurt, and the older of the men grabbed her by the hair and turned her face into the light.

'It's a lassie!' he exclaimed. 'Well, fancy that! Even the women are taking up poaching!'

The younger man was thrashing around in the bushes, poking at them with his gun barrel, and suddenly he gave a cry of triumph and knelt down, picking up a bundle from under a bush.

He brought it over and held it in front of the light. The bundle comprised about eight dead rabbits, strung on a thin wire.

'Aye, we caught her nicely,' the younger man said. 'Before she could pick up the night's bag.'

'I'm not a poacher!' Fiona cried, struggling in the older gamekeeper's grip. 'I'm from New Zealand. I'm staying with friends near Duntochter.'

The older man tightened his grip on her hair as he studied her dirty face and muddy sweater and jeans. 'A likely story,' he growled. 'And by what right are you inside the Castle grounds?'

'I—I was visiting somebody—Mr Ross, the American who's living at the cottage. Old Wullie at the gate knows me.'

'Och aye! And what were you doing running about in the dark in the woods?' His voice was heavy with scepticism.

'I—I—oh, I was running away!'

He grunted, 'We ken that.'

The younger man said, 'She's telling lies, Mr McKechnie. She's with the poachers. They must be using a woman because they think we'll let her off lightly.'

McKechnie nodded. 'I wouldn't put it past them, Georgie. Anyway——' he tightened his grip on her hair—'it's up to the castle with you. We'll hand you over to Sir Angus and you can tell him your story.'

Fiona struggled. 'I don't want to go to the Castle! Take me to Wullie's cottage. He can tell you who I am.'

McKechnie shook his head. 'Naw, we'll take you up to Sir Angus. Then he'll know we're on the job. So start marching!'

He released her hair and prodded her with the shotgun and she stumbled forward. With prods of the gun he directed her through the woods and, tight-lipped and seething, Fiona let herself be forced ahead of them.

They came out of the woods near the track to Gordon's cottage and she stopped abruptly and said curtly, 'You could go and ask Mr Ross about me. He'll tell you I'm not a poacher.'

McKechnie looked at her dubiously for a minute. Then he growled, 'All right, Georgie, run up to the cottage and ask about her. I'll keep her here until you get back.'

She stood silently while the younger man strode up the track to Gordon's cottage.

He was back within a few minutes and shook his head. 'There's nobody there,' he said.

Fiona opened her mouth to tell them that Gordon had probably driven down to the gate, no doubt with the aim of catching her when she tried to leave the estate. But the two gamekeepers didn't give her a chance. 'On you go,' McKechnie ordered, prodding her with the gun. 'Up to the Castle.'

She thought sullenly that the sooner they got to the Castle the sooner this whole farce would be over. However much he disliked her, Sir Angus knew she wasn't a poacher, or in league with the poachers.

The two gamekeepers kept her moving through

the rain at a brisk pace until they reached the
turreted pile of the ancient Castle and walked
across a sweeping carriageway to the portico, then
up broad stone steps to the ornate iron-studded
double doors. McKechnie tugged on a big old-
fashioned bell that hung by the door, and eventually one door was flung open and a grey-haired
man wearing the apparel of a butler looked out at
them.

'Evening, Fergus,' said McKechnie. 'We've
caught a poacher and we want to hand her over to
Sir Angus.'

The old butler glanced at Fiona with distaste,
his eyes sliding over her muddy figure and strag-
gling hair.

'Aye, bring her in,' he said curtly.

Fiona was pushed into the huge entrance hall
with its panelled timber walls and gilt-framed
pictures which were interspersed with stags'
heads, shields, claymores and tapestries.

The butler said, 'Keep her here, McKechnie,
and I'll tell Sir Angus.'

He shuffled across the stone-flagged floor,
stopped outside a double, glass-panelled door
then knocked and paused and went in. Nothing
happened for a few minutes, then the glass-
panelled doors were flung open and, black beard
bristling, Sir Angus strode out. He was wearing a
tweed suit and his brow was dark as he strode
towards Fiona and his gamekeepers.

McKechnie touched his cap as Sir Angus
stopped a few paces away from Fiona and glared
at her.

'You found her poaching?' he barked.

'Aye, we did, sir,' the younger gamekeeper said, holding up the bundle of rabbits. 'This was her night's bag.'

Sir Angus glared at her. 'I know you, don't I? I met you at the dance. And my daughter said you were one of the radicals who mucked up my deer shoot. Then I saw you at the ceremony this afternoon—with Charles Stewart and his rabble. And now you've been caught poaching in my estate. You're an absolute hooligan, girl—to say nothing of being a thief!'

Fiona said spiritedly, 'I wasn't poaching. I was visiting Mr Ross in his cottage.'

Sir Angus looked at McKechnie, who shook his head. 'We caught her in the grounds, sir. She was running away. We think she was going to collect the rabbits.'

Sir Angus nodded. 'That's good enough for me. Bundle her in a car and take her into Duntochter and tell MacGregor to lock her up. And tell him I'll be pressing charges.'

Fiona stamped her foot. 'This is ridiculous! I'm not a poacher! I'm a visitor, here on holiday. I'm not a thief!'

Behind Sir Angus, Moyra emerged from the glass-panelled doors and strolled towards them.

Fiona glanced at her and said heatedly, 'Your daughter knows I'm not a poacher!'

Moyra halted near Sir Angus and glanced venomously over Fiona's muddy, bedraggled figure. 'I'm not too sure that she's speaking the truth,' she said icily. 'I know she's not above poaching—or trying to take things that don't belong to her. I think you're doing the right thing, Father. A night in jail would do her the world of good.'

Sir Angus grunted, 'I agree.'

From outside there was a squeal of brakes as a car pulled up, and Fiona glared at Moyra's sardonically smiling face and snapped, 'You're horrible! You know I——'

Behind her, feet sounded on the flagstones and Sir Angus glanced over her shoulder and said shortly, 'Hello, Gordon.'

Fiona refused to look round, but was aware of Gordon striding up and standing beside her. She looked straight ahead as Gordon said, 'Evening, Sir Angus.'

Sir Angus said, 'This—girl—was caught poaching. She claims you invited her to your cottage.'

Gordon said nothing for a moment and she could feel him looking at her. She thought furiously, the beast, he's going to say he didn't ask me to his cottage and let me be taken to jail. Ask me—he abducted me!

But Gordon nodded and said, 'I did invite her. But she left in a hurry.' He glanced coldly at Fiona. 'But I don't think she's a poacher.'

'Hmm!' Sir Angus snorted, 'she looks grubby enough to be one. And she's made an absolute nuisance of herself. At the deer shoot—and today at the ceremony with her rabble-rousing friends. I'd like to charge her with something.'

Gordon said, 'I'll take her home. I agree she's a nuisance.'

'A pest!' Moyra added coldly.

Gordon took Fiona's arm, but she pulled herself free. 'I'll get home by myself!' she snapped.

'You'll be escorted off my estate!' Sir Angus bellowed. 'And I'll thank you, Gordon, not to invite her back again!'

'He didn't invite me!' Fiona cried. 'He dragged me here! It's the last place in Scotland I wanted to come to!'

Sir Angus glared at her, then jerked his head at his gamekeepers. 'Take her to the gate!' he snapped. 'And throw her off my property!'

The two gamekeepers moved forward, but before they could touch her Gordon seized her by the arm and spun her round, then half forced, half dragged her out of the hall. She quivered with fury, but let him take her through the big doors, down the steps and across to the Land Rover.

The two gamekeepers followed and McKechnie called out, 'Beg pardon, sir, but Sir Angus wants us to see the young lady off the property.'

Gordon nodded as he wrenched the passenger door open. 'Get in the back,' he said. 'I'll drop you off at the gate.'

The light misty rain had become quite heavy and the two gamekeepers were glad to scramble into the back of the car. Gordon switched on the windshield wipers, then drove down the long drive.

Fiona sat and silently seethed, huddled as far away from Gordon as she could get. Nobody tried to make any conversation until they reached the gates when he stopped the car and waited while the two gamekeepers got out of the rear door.

'Thank you, sir,' McKechnie called, waving his shotgun.

Gordon nodded, then he muttered a sudden oath as Fiona opened her door and slid swiftly out into the rain.

'Goodbye!' she shouted, staring at him behind the wheel. 'I'll walk home by myself! And don't try to follow me, or I'll run into the woods and hide!'

He stared at her, his face dark and glowering in the light from the dashboard.

'You are a stupid, dumb girl!' he ground out. 'I'm tired of trying to stop you doing dopey things!'

'And I'm tired of you bullying me!' she cried. 'I just wish I was a man! I—I'd show you!'

He slammed the car into gear and said disgustedly, 'Go on, walk home and get soaked. Catch pneumonia and spend the rest of your holiday in bed. That's what I'd expect from you.'

'My holiday's over!' she snapped. 'I'm leaving tomorrow. Goodbye!'

She turned and strode out through the gate, past old Wullie, who raised his eyebrows and saluted her.

The gatekeeper took his pipe from his mouth, then shuffled over to the Land Rover and looked in the passenger door. He glanced up at Gordon, who was hunched over the wheel staring bleakly after Fiona's retreating, quivering figure as she vanished into the night.

Old Wullie said, 'She's a fair handful, that lassie.' Gordon grunted and Wullie said admiringly, 'But she's a bonnie wee fighter. If I were twenty years younger I'd even try and tame her myself.'

Gordon growled, 'You'd be wasting your time. She's as stubborn as a mule and has even less brain. I'm glad to see the last of her!'

CHAPTER TWELVE

IN spite of Gordon's dire forebodings that she would catch pneumonia by refusing a ride and walking through the rain, Fiona suffered no ill effects from her hectic day, during which just about everything seemed to have happened. She had come close to being arrested at the protest; she had been abducted by that brute, Gordon, then bundled into his bed and almost seduced; she had been caught by the gamekeepers and marched at gunpoint to the Castle to face the wrath of Sir Angus; then finally, through choice, she had strode out of the Castle gates to face a two-mile walk home through the soaking rain.

Nothing else can happen to me now, she thought miserably as she squelched her way along the dark country road, wondering if she should risk hitching a ride with the first vehicle that came along. She felt that things must start improving—she'd had more than enough tribulations for one day.

Her bulky sweater was almost soaked through and her long red hair was plastered over her face. Even her stout brogues were waterlogged from splashing through puddles when she had fled into the Castle grounds. Cold rain began to trickle down her back and she shivered and fought back a sneeze. She hoped desperately she wouldn't catch a cold and not be able to travel tomorrow

on the train to London. There was no way she
would stay in the Highlands another day and risk
seeing Gordon Ross again. She'd had enough of
him! Her life had been a mess since she met him—
a series of violent ups and downs.

It would have been different if she could have
believed he regarded her as anything but a mere
plaything. But she knew she had been deluding
herself when she had thought—hoped—that perhaps he felt something for her. Something more
than a desire for another conquest. But, she
scolded herself, it had been her own fault. Because
he had been so eager to spend most of his time
with her, she had assumed he was falling for her,
as she had certainly fallen for him. But it had been
one-sided. To him she had only been a distraction—that was his word. A distraction and an
amusing diversion from the sophisticated Moyra.

As she squelched on she thought she should be
thankful. At least she had found out about him in
time and not thrown herself away on a jet-setting
philanderer. She wondered how many young girls
he had seduced during his world travels. Plenty,
she thought. Being a photographer made it easy
for him to attract starry-eyed girls and have his
fill of them. There must be an endless supply of
girls like her who were overwhelmed by his experienced, man-of-the-world wooing—until he
moved on and forgot about them.

She sneezed suddenly and muttered furiously
that she was not going to catch a cold and give
him the satisfaction of being right. Then, behind
her, the road was lit by the headlights of a car and

she stopped and turned to face it. For a moment she thought it might be Gordon coming after her, and her heart began to pound. She wouldn't be able to stand another confrontation with him. She was too tired, wet and miserable. But as the car approached and then slowed she saw it was a sports car. Then as it pulled up beside her she saw it was Charles' MG.

He jumped out and exclaimed, 'Fiona! What are you doing here?'

She shivered. 'I'm wet. And cold. I'll tell you in the car.'

He wrenched the door open and she tumbled in out of the rain. Charles got in and drove on.

He told her briefly he was on his way home from the village where he had been celebrating with the other protesters, but he was more concerned about her and bombarded her with questions. She gave him a garbled story about how she had been rescued from the thick of the demonstration—by Gordon Ross—and taken to the Castle. Charles said he had been concerned about her and had phoned his mother, who told him Fiona had phoned to say she was all right and was with friends. She sidetracked him by asking how the protest had gone and he told her in detail until they reached Elgin House.

Mrs Stewart tut-tutted when she saw the soaked and bedraggled Fiona and ordered her to get out of her wet clothes while she prepared a hot mustard bath. After a long soak in the steaming, pungent bath, Fiona once again received Jessie's home cold cure of ginger, cinnamon, sugar, hot water and malt whisky, then was bundled off to bed. Next morning she woke with a slightly thick head, but no trace of a cold.

During the morning, she packed for her journey to London, while Jessie fussed around telling her how upset she was that Fiona couldn't stay any longer. At lunch time, Fiona gave her several presents she had brought from London. Later, just before she went out of the house to get into Charles' car for the drive to Inverness, she handed Jessie the volume of Burns' poems that Gordon had given her.

As she got into the car she thought, so that disposes of my only tangible reminder of Gordon Ross!

Then she remembered the pictures of her he had taken and which were packed in her bag. She supposed she would always keep them; they were too good to throw away.

They were driving towards Inverness, Fiona lost in thought, when she remembered that although she had plenty of pictures of herself—taken by him—she didn't have a single photo of him.

Just as well, she thought grimly. I don't expect I'll ever see him again, so forgetting him should be easy.

At the station, Charles carried her two suitcases on board the express train to London via Edinburgh, and in her compact first class sleeping compartment she sat on the day bed while he stowed her cases.

They had arrived at Inverness station with plenty of time to spare—thanks to Mrs Stewart.

Jessie was the kind of traveller who believed a person never properly caught a train unless they were at the station at least an hour before departure time. Now they had half an hour to fill before the train left on its long overnight trip to London.

Charles opened the window, then leaned out and peered along the busy platform, giving Fiona a running commentary on arriving passengers and the people seeing them off. She sat on her bed and tried to respond to his small talk. She looked very attractive in a short classic jacket in pale grey herringbone with a shawl collar. Under it she wore a cream silk shirt open at the throat and her short skirt was in grey flannel.

Charles chatted away about the people who would be her fellow travellers and about the train's route which ran down the east coast of Scotland and England. When she had arrived in Inverness Fiona had come on the west coast route. Charles had done the trip via Edinburgh many times and he told her the dining car service was rather good.

'They don't serve meals in the sleeping compartments,' he said, 'but I've reserved a seat in the dining car for you.'

There was a sudden flash of light farther along the platform and Charles craned his neck out of the window, then said, 'Must be a celebrity leaving. Some press photographer is taking pictures.' Then he turned to Fiona and grimaced, 'It's Moyra Deardon. She must be going to Edinburgh. I read in the paper that she's the star model in a big wool promotion there next week.'

He glanced at her and said wryly, 'I don't expect you'll go out of your way to meet her during the journey.'

Fiona forced a smile. She was sure Moyra would have little desire to talk with her either.

'She's got a lot of luggage,' Charles said, leaning out of the window. 'About ten suitcases. I can see why she's going by train. Although I believe she hates flying.'

He got up and glanced at his watch. 'Well, nearly departure time. I'll get off now and stand at the window until the train pulls out.'

Fiona got up and he took her in his arms and kissed her awkwardly. 'Until I see you again,' he said. 'Which I hope will be soon.'

She nodded and squeezed his hand. 'Thanks for all your hospitality. I really appreciated everything.'

He smiled. 'Next time you come to the Highlands, I hope it'll be for much longer.'

He left the compartment, then went out on to the platform where he stood by her window and held her hand until the long train began to glide from the platform. He released her hand and called, 'Goodbye, Fiona.'

She waved and blew him a kiss, then far back along the platform, near the ticket gate, she saw a tall, fair-haired man in a duffle coat tear through the barrier and race along the platform until he just managed to swing himself athletically through a door of the last carriage. Her heart pounded when she saw it was Gordon.

She slumped back in the seat, distraught, and

wondered feverishly what he was doing taking this train. Then, as her heart stopped racing, she realised he must be going to Edinburgh—with Moyra. But obviously Gordon wasn't the type who left himself time to spare when he caught a train.

She abandoned her plans to go to the restaurant car and have a pre-dinner drink. It had been bad enough knowing Moyra was on board and that she might see her. Now, with Gordon on board too, it was worse. She might see them together.

She decided she would stay in her compartment until after the train reached Edinburgh and they both got off. It meant she would miss dinner, but she should be able to get some kind of snack after Edinburgh.

She had planned to have dinner, then come back and change into her night things and go to bed. But now she would have to stay awake until after Edinburgh. She felt very cross about that, for she always slept well on trains—the motion lulled her to sleep very quickly. And sleep was something she badly needed, for she had hardly had any since she had met Gordon. But there was no way she was going to walk through to the restaurant car and risk seeing the two of them.

About an hour out of Inverness there was a light tap on her door and a broad Scots voice called, 'Tickets, please, ma'am.'

She opened the door and the inspector took her ticket and examined it, then handed it back. He called her by name, and she saw he held a passenger list clipped to a board.

She asked him to cancel her dinner reservation,

saying she didn't feel hungry. 'Aye, Miss Cameron,' he said affably, 'I'll do that. But you'll be very hungry by breakfast time tomorrow.'

She tried to read a book to while away the hours as the train sped south. It was dark outside, so there was little to see, with only a brief stop at Perth to break the monotony.

She dozed in her seat, forcing herself not to think about Gordon and Moyra somewhere on the train.

Before Edinburgh, she drew the blinds so there was no chance of them seeing her as they left the train. She kept the blinds drawn until the train began its journey again after the Edinburgh stop. Then she released the blinds and stared out into the night as the train gathered speed for the long haul to London.

She was contemplating going to the restaurant car to try and get a snack when there was a tap on the door and a Scots-accented voiced called out, 'Tickets please, ma'am.'

She sighed and got her ticket from her bag and opened the door.

Gordon stood there in his duffle coat and he looked at her coldly before moving quickly into the compartment and closing the door behind him. Fiona stumbled back and cried, 'What—what are you doing here? I thought you got off at Edinburgh—with—with Moyra.'

He shook his head. 'Moyra got off at Edinburgh. I didn't know she was on the train until I met her at the bar. I'm going to London.'

'Oh,' she said, backing towards the window.

'What—what are you going there for?'

'That's an interesting question,' he said evenly. 'Visiting London wasn't in my plans.'

'Then why did you change them? Not that I care!' she added, tossing her head.

He smiled grimly. 'I phoned Elgin House to talk with you. Mrs Stewart told me you'd left for Inverness to take this train. So I took it too—and caught it by the skin of my teeth.'

He slipped off his duffle coat and tossed it on her bed. Then he sat down and put his feet up on the facing seat. 'You're pretty comfortable here,' he commented. 'I couldn't get a sleeper—they're all full. So I may have to sit up all night.'

'I'm sure you won't be too uncomfortable,' she said shortly.

'I haven't even got a toothbrush. No bags either. Only what I stand up in.' He looked at her. 'You wouldn't be carrying a spare toothbrush?'

'No,' she said curtly, 'I'm not.'

'Well,' he drawled, 'maybe I can share yours, in the morning.'

Her face flamed. 'No, you won't!' she cried. 'And you can just get out of here or I'll call——'

He stood up from the bed and had his arms round her before she could say any more. Fiona struggled, but he drew her down on the bed and kissed her until her struggles subsided.

'You've caused me a heap of trouble,' he murmured, 'But when I hear you say you love me it will have been worth while.'

'Love you!' she spluttered, trying to avoid his lips, 'I—I——'

Gordon held her chin firmly in one hand and gazed into her eyes. 'I love you, Fiona. I just didn't want to admit it—even to myself. But when I realised I might never see you again, that was it. You've bewitched me—and I love you very much.'

'Oh!' She stared up at him. 'I—I thought you were only playing with me. I thought—you and Moyra—I thought you were going to Edinburgh with her.'

He shook his head. 'Everything between Moyra and me was over before I got to Scotland. I made that clear to her last night after you went—and I told her what I thought of her for sneaking her things into my cottage hoping you'd find them.'

'And I—I fell for it,' Fiona muttered.

'I don't blame you. Moyra's pretty ruthless. And that's not the kind of girl I want to marry. I want to marry you.'

He kissed her tenderly and she gave a huge sigh as she melted into his arms.

He tilted her head and murmured, 'Well, will you be my wife? Share my cabin? Cook for me? Have our babies?'

Fiona sighed and her face radiated happiness.

'Oh, yes,' she smiled, 'I will. I'll do all these things. And I'll love you for ever and ever.'

Gordon looked deep into her eyes, then he smiled and said, 'I know you'll love and honour me—but will you *obey*?'

'Yes,' she sighed, 'I will, my darling.'

Her arms entwined themselves round his neck and there was no way he could see her tightly-crossed fingers.

Harlequin® Plus

A FAVORITE SCOTTISH DISH

Highland's Rapture takes place in the highlands of Scotland, where Fiona and Gordon enjoy the culinary specialities of the area. Among other dishes, they eat cock-a-leekie soup. This odd-sounding concoction is a traditional and tasty Scottish recipe, and we thought readers might like to try it for themselves.

What you need:

  1 3-4 lb. broiler chicken
  12 cups cold water
  7 leeks, washed, trimmed and diced
  2/3 cup rice, uncooked
  1 tbsp. salt
  pepper to taste
  3/4 lb. pitted prunes, chopped
  1/2 cup chopped parsley

What to do:

Wash chicken thoroughly and place in a large saucepan. Add water, bring to a boil and skim. Add leeks, rice, salt and pepper. Partially cover saucepan and simmer for approximately 2 hours. Add prunes and simmer another 30 minutes. Remove chicken from soup and separate from bones, then dice and return meat to soup. Before serving, garnish with chopped parsley. Delicious!